Suddenly, something caught at Melissa's ankles and pulled her under the water!

She kicked and kicked to free herself from whatever was clinging to her. For one moment she managed to kick free and went shooting to the surface, calling for help. Then the groping tentacles gripped her ankles once again and she was pulled down, down into the dark waters. . . .

Then, as suddenly as it began, it was over. Whatever had wrapped around Melissa's legs slipped away, and she rose to the surface, as her friends swam to her aid.

Later, Melissa sat on the beach with Jake. "Look," she said, "you can still see the marks on my ankles where the seaweed tangled around them."

"I didn't notice them before," said Jake, looking more closely. He began to appear puzzled and worried.

"But what kind of a weed," he said finally, "would leave impressions like finger prints?"

Myrtle For My Love

by

DAISY THOMSON

PYRAMID BOOKS ▲ NEW YORK

MYRTLE FOR MY LOVE

A PYRAMID BOOK

First published in Great Britain 1977
Pyramid edition published July 1977

Printed in the United States of America

Pyramid Books are published by Pyramid Publications (Harcourt Brace Jovanovich, Inc.). Its trademarks, consisting of the
word "Pyramid" and the portrayal of a pyramid, are registered
in the United States Patent Office.

Pyramid Publications
(Harcourt Brace Jovanovich, Inc.)
757 Third Avenue, New York, N. Y. 10017

ONE

I slipped the boarding pass into the easily accessible outer compartment of my handbag, picked up my small, scarlet cabin case, and strolled across to the airport bookstall to select a novel which would occupy my attention during the two hour flight to Sardinia.

I could not help smiling to myself as I crossed the busy hall of the terminal building, where passengers of differing nationalities were milling around, looking for luggage trolleys, or information centers, or merely somewhere to sit.

Even at this late stage, I could not quite believe that instead of flying home, from Milan to London, in a few minutes I would be boarding a plane bound for Alghero, where I would spend the next two months with my Uncle Max and his team of archaeologists, a team which on this occasion also included his god-son, Jonathan Angus Carnegie, called Jake for short.

At the thought of Jake, my blood warmed with a pleasurable sensation of delight, and my smile became even wider, only to be switched off abruptly when it was hopefully and leeringly returned by a tall, over-handsome, over-sleek, over-well-dressed man, who was standing beside the postcard whirligig near the counter, idly pushing it round and round.

I flushed with annoyance as the man continued to ogle me with hopeful interest, and patently avoiding his gaze, I hurried past him, and concentrated my attention on the display of paperback books on the stall.

As I picked up the nearest one to read the blurb, I heard a woman's low, amused voice murmur in English, "Really, Danny! Can't you keep your mind off pretty girls for just a few moments, while we discuss business?"

The man's amused laugh irritated me as he replied, "I can combine pleasure with business any day, and she is a pretty little thing, isn't she?"

The hairs at the nape of my neck bristled with indignation at his tone, although I doubted if they would have spoken about me within my earshot, had they realized I was a fellow countrywoman.

"You will be baby snatching next!" the woman sneered.

The man laughed again. "You should talk, my dear! You are the one with that in mind!"

"For heaven's sake, Danny!" the low voice hissed in anger.

"Sorry, my dear," the man chuckled, "but you did ask for it, you know!"

"Forget the chit, and talk business!" she reprimanded him. "I do not have any time to waste, Danny. The others will be wondering where I have got to!"

"And of course, it would never do for you to be seen talking to a tall, dark and handsome young man, would it?" he mocked, but although he was addressing a woman who was out of my sight on the other side of the postcard stand, I had the unpleasant feeling that the suave Danny was still eyeing me with his blue, flirtative eyes, more interested in me than in her, although I kept my back turned to him.

"No!" the woman replied to his riposte. "It would not do if we were seen together, and you know it, so listen, please!"

"Very well," he sighed. "You want me to confirm that I can be at The Pink Grotto at three o'clock sharp on the 7th of July—a fortnight from today, to be exact, at which time you, looking blonde and beautiful, will arrive with the boy, am I right?"

"Yes, quite right!" said the woman curtly, "but remember—"

Whatever else she was going to say I did not hear, for my attention was distracted by a voice over the loudspeaker system, which was announcing that my flight to Alghero was now boarding.

I hurriedly picked up a couple of Italian fashion magazines and a paperback translation into Italian of a Gothic romance by a well known English writer. I was in the right frame of mind for such a tale, for it would make quite a change from the classical books I had been reading recently.

I paid the cashier, tucked my purchases under my arm, and walked away from the counter in the direction of the passport control desk.

I could not avoid walking past the postcard rack, but as I drew level with it, I instinctively gave a surreptitious glance towards it, not so much to see if the suave Englishman was still standing there, as to catch a glimpse of the woman to whom he had been talking.

The man was no longer there, and I very much doubted if the stout little woman in the well worn, tight-fitting, black costume, whose untidy bun looked in danger of unwinding at any minute, was the woman whose soft voice I had overheard only minutes earlier.

Since it was the beginning of the summer season, and since Sardinia is popular as a holiday haunt, the plane was filled to capacity, and I found myself at the tail end of a long line of tourist class passengers who were waiting to board the DC9 through its rear door, while the handful of passengers who were traveling first class disappeared into the front entrance.

The seat I had been allocated was about half way down the plane, next to a porthole, and when I reached it, I took off the tailored jacket of my new cord trouser suit, folded it neatly and stowed it into the overhead locker, before sidling into my seat.

As I fastened my seat belt, ready for take off, I smiled politely at the elderly couple who were seating themselves alongside me, before sitting back comfortably in the high-backed chair and allowing myself to relax completely for the first time in months.

As I closed my eyes, I thought how wonderful it was not to be rushing around, keeping a watchful eye on a score of high-spirited and very spoiled young women. It was wonderful to have no one to consider for the next few hours, except myself. Above all, it was wonderful how this unexpected working holiday, which I suspected would be more holiday than work, had cropped up.

For the past few weeks, Max Little, my mother's youngest brother, had been working with a team of enthusiastic young archaeologists on a site in Sardinia, and for the duration of their stay on the island, Max had rented a large villa on the outskirts of Alghero, which was big enough to accommodate himself and all the members of his team. Everything had gone well until the cook-housekeeper he had hired had been lured away by one of the new holiday hotels, which could pay her a much higher wage than Max could afford.

Jane Hunter, the only woman member of the team, had tried to cope with the cooking, but this hadn't worked

As my uncle wrote in his letter,

"Although Jane's cooking does not seem too bad to me, Jake, and Leo, her brother, and my other two young assistants are rebelling against it.

"When I mentioned this in a letter to your mother, she wrote back to me to say that since you were giving up your post at this school in Montreux towards the end of June, and had nothing planned before taking up your post in St. Andrews in October, you might be interested in helping us out, so how about it, Melissa? How about spending two months of comparative idleness here, in the sunshine of this fascinating island?

"All we would expect of you is that you would make breakfast, provide a packed lunch, and have dinner ready for us when we come home in the evening? A young girl comes in at night for a couple of hours to do the washing up and the housework, so you see, you would have plenty of free time. All your expenses would be paid, but I'm afraid the salary I can offer is minimal. However, should you wish to augment it, you could get the job of tutoring the small boy who lives next door to us for a few hours each morning, on general subjects. Again, there would not be much work attached to this job, since his mother merely wants someone to keep him out of the way for an hour or so, with not too much emphasis on the educational side.

"He is a bright, intelligent, eight year old, and I think you would enjoy working with him.

"I told Sally, his mother, that if you did consider taking on the job, you would not want to start right away, for I thought you might like a fortnight away from the atmosphere of the schoolroom, before undertaking another stint of teaching."

Max's large, bold handwriting had flowed over page after page, to convince me of how much I would enjoy living in Sardinia, telling me that there were lots of interesting little towns to explore, beautiful scenery, good bathing, and lots of night life in Alghero, but it was the fact that his god-son Jake was one of this team, which had decided the issue for me.

Thinking about Jake, I smiled to myself again, as I had smiled to myself in the airport terminal. Jake and I have known each other since I could crawl. He is five years older than me, and, unfortunately, he can remember some of the stupid, infantile things I used to do—things which I would rather he forgot about, for there are times when, to tease me, he repeats these silly antics of mine to my friends, and more particularly of recent years, to the young men who came to take me out.

We had grown up in the same small town in Scotland, argued, fought, stood up for each other and maligned each other, much as brother and sister do, until Jake had gone off to the university, and then somehow, things were never quite the same.

He was a man, I was an adolescent schoolgirl, and how I resented the difference in our years then, particularly when he brought home, as he did from time to time, his current love, who was invariably slim, tall and dark-haired, elegantly fragile looking, with liquid brown eyes, sophisticated clothes and sophisticated manners, which all emphasised the fact that I was small and, at that time, plumpish; more at home in old jeans and a shapeless pullover; a tow-headed tomboy of a girl, whose tip-tilted nose speckled unbecomingly with brown freckles at the first hint of summer sun.

After graduating from the university, Jake had worked abroad as a geologist with an oil company, and for the past years our holidays had never coincided, so that although we scrawled each other an occasional letter, and I heard news of him from Max, we had not seen each other, and I was anxious to know if he had changed much, and, what was more important, what he would think of me, now that I was grown up, and well beyond the adolescent stage of freckles and scruffy jeans.

I was so lost in my pleasant dreams that I left my novel unopened on my knee, and I did not realize how much time had passed until I heard the captain's voice announce that we were about to

11

land at Alghero, and would we please fasten our seat belts and put out our cigarettes.

Before fastening my seat belt, I craned my neck to look out through the porthole for my first sight of the ancient island kingdom of Sardinia.

Daylight was swiftly giving way to nightfall, and all I could see was a sea of deep, deep purple, dark as the heart of a pansy, then a winking light of welcome from a white lighthouse on the top of a promontory which jutted darkly into the purple sea, and a jagged, irregular coastline traced out in the white froth of the waves which washed against the cliffs. We flew on, over the land, and I could dimly make out the shapes of weird round hills, different from any hills I had ever seen, hills that looked as if they should belong to some strange planet, not to this world of ours, and for a frightened moment, panic gripped at my throat, and I could not breathe, could not swallow the saliva of fear which filled my mouth and for a frightening moment, it seemed to me that my future was going to be as strangely dark and menacing as these unfamiliar hills over which the airliner was banking for a final turn before coming in to land.

I gave an uncontrollable shiver, which caused the elderly woman seated beside me to turn to me with a sympathetic gaze. She took my hand and gave it a reassuring pat before fastening my seat belt for me and saying, in an Italian dialect which I found difficult to follow,

"Do not be afraid, signorina. We have made this trip many times, and always we have landed safely!"

She patted my hand again, and continued to

talk to me reassuringly, giving me time to pull myself together, giving me time to overcome the unexpected moment of panic, when for an unpredictable reason I had wished that I was on board a London bound plane, on the first stage of my homeward journey to Scotland, instead of on this foreign airliner, which was bringing me to a strange land, to the ancient island which is said to have been created in the shape of a footstep of one of the gods; to an island whose myths and legends date to long before the Christian era, and whose very place names betray its associations with the gods of antiquity.

TWO

By the time the plane had landed and taxied along the runway to come to a halt on the apron in front of the air terminal building, my strange mood of impending doom had totally evaporated, and as I followed the other passengers down the central passage of the DC9 to the gangway steps, I laughed at myself for letting my overvivid imagination run away with me.

I told myself that the moment of panic had been engendered not by precognition of some fearful fate which lay in wait for me, but by the sheer excitement of knowing that very soon I would be seeing Jake again, and hoping, yes, hoping very fervently, that he would not see me through yesterday's eyes, as the gawky, prickly young person I had been at our last meeting, but through eyes that would appreciate that I was now a pretty and self-confident young woman, with no traces of the former tomboy in either looks or comportment.

The last glimmers of daylight had almost completely vanished in the minutes it had taken the plane to come down to land, and as I stepped out onto the gangway, I paused for a moment to appreciate, as I have always appreciated, the lovely bluish glow which illuminates Mediterranean lands at the brief period of twilight.

The evening air was still pleasantly warm, and as I walked across the strip to the entrance of airport arrival hall, the smell of hot engine oil and paraffin fumes was borne away from me on a lusty gust from the surrounding hills, and in their place, my nostrils scented the sweet smell of the maquis which the breeze was carrying from the bosky slopes. Once again my blood stirred with excitement, but this time the excitement I experienced was a pleasant one, for the mingled smells of the mountain herbs reminded me of pleasant holidays I had spent in the South of France, and made me think that my coming holiday would no doubt be equally pleasant.

I reached the luggage arrival point, and stood impatiently at the wooden trestle table, waiting for my case to be unloaded from the plane. Every now and then, I rose on my tiptoes, to peer over the heads of my fellow travelers toward the reception hall which lay beyond the customs and passport control barrier, in the hope of spotting among the crowd of people assembled there to greet their friends, a sight of my tall uncle.

In his letter, thanking me for undertaking to help him out as cook for his team, Max had said that he would come to the airport to meet me and drive me to the villa which he had rented, since there was not a bus service which passed near to it, but although Max is over six feet tall, with a thatch of dark, usually untidy hair and a black, piratical-looking beard, so that he tends to stand out in any crowd, I could not see him anywhere

16

among the groups of people waiting beyond the barrier.

I retrieved my luggage from the table and passed without fuss through customs control and the passport desk, where a handsome young Sard gave me an appreciative look as he glanced from my passport photograph to me, and gallantly wished me a happy holiday in Alghero. However, I paid scant attention to him, as my anxious gaze again swept around the arrival hall, and again I failed to spot Max.

I sighed with annoyance. Max is not a clock watcher, and if he had become involved in an interesting project, it was quite possible that he had forgotten he was due to meet me at the airport.

I walked dejectedly across the small hall. Should I wait outside, hanging around the airport, in case Max was even now on his way to meet me, or should I take the airport bus, which was about to leave, to the town center, and from there, hope to find a taxi which would take me to the Villa Gelsomino?

As I stood hesitant at the exit, biting my underlip in indecision, a cheerful voice hailed me.

"Melissa! It is you! I almost did not recognise you!"

I spun round, smiling with relief and delight to see Jake Carnegie, grinning from ear to ear, looking a little more lean-faced than before, and very much more suntanned, so that his blue eyes seemed even bluer than I remembered them, come striding towards me, followed by Leo Hunter.

"Jake!" I dropped my cases as he enveloped me

17

in a warm hug of welcome. "Jake!" I repeated. "It is good to see you again!"

I wriggled from his grip, and holding him at arm's length smiled up at him. "You haven't changed one little bit!" I beamed.

"You have, Melissa!" he chuckled. "It's no wonder that I did not recognize you at first! No puppy-fat! No tousled hair or two! No ancient jeans! No out-of-the-toe sneakers!"

I laughed.

"What a memory to have of me, Jake!" I shook my head. "But tell me," I turned back to him after returning Leo's welcoming kiss, "why isn't Max here? He said he would be, and I was looking out for him, and not for your welcoming committee!"

"Max doesn't enjoy driving, Italian style," explained Jake. "He says he is getting too old for the cut and thrust of Roman chariot racing, as he calls it, getting his metaphors mixed as usual, so Leo and I offered to meet you instead."

Jake looked at me again, admiration in his eyes, and shook his head.

"I still can't believe it is really you, Melissa! Do you remember the last time I saw you? It was a pouring wet day, and I had come to the hockey grounds, to say goodbye to you, before going south. You were coming off the pitch, with mud galore over your clothes, your face, your hair, and—" he turned to Leo, still grinning, "would you believe it, she had the audacity to rush up to me and give me a fond farewell kiss! Myrna was not at all amused, I remember, and I somehow got the feeling that you had done it deliberately," he smiled at me.

Myrna had been his girl friend at that time, and looking at him now, seeing how much handsomer he had become, how much more sure of himself, I could not help wondering how many other Myrnas there had been in his life since then, and if, indeed, there was a special woman in his life at this moment.

Leo was eyeing me with interest.

"You may have slimmed down, Melissa, and I like your Italian style trouser suit, but in spite of it, you still don't look much more than a schoolgirl. So tell me," he asked, "how on earth did you manage to keep your finishing school pupils in order, when you could pass for one of them yourself?"

I laughed. Leo was an old friend of Jake's, and I was used to his teasing from way back. "I wore granny spectacles," I told him, "and I put my hair up in a tight bun, painted on wrinkles and wore the highest heels I could find so that my pupils would not look down on me—"

I bent down to pick up my cases as I was speaking, but Leo forestalled me.

"In spite of your air of independence, Melissa," he said, "and in spite of women's lib and all that, I like to act the gallant cavalier where a pretty girl is concerned." He picked up the cases as though they were feather light.

Jake tucked my arm into his. "Don't let Leo's remarks go to your head, Melissa," he warned. "Nowadays he pays compliments to every girl. Although he has not acquired much of their language, he has acquired an Italian talent for

19

successfully chatting to the female sex since he came here!"

"I like it!" I smiled at Leo. "It makes a pleasant change to be cosseted, after being the one who had to cosset a score or so of spoilt and temperamental young women for over a year!"

"You must tell me about this school you were teaching at," said Jake, as we followed Leo, who was weaving his way past the groups still waiting outside the airport for the arrival of their friends, or for transport to take them to their destinations.

"There is so much to tell, I don't know where to begin!" I smiled.

The light from the electric lamps stretching out over the barrel-shaped palm trees which lined the square in front of the airport, highlighted the brilliance of the fern green leaves and the gaudy colors of the salvias and hibiscus which grew in the beds surrounding them.

I stopped for a moment to admire a clump of deep red canna lilies whose heads nodded lazily in the light evening breeze, just as Leo, too, came to a halt, but it wasn't to look at the lilies that he had stopped. He was smiling admiringly at a slim young woman, with shoulder-length, copper-colored hair which gleamed like fine silk under the arc lights, who was about to step into a large white Mercedes.

Jake's grasp on my arm tightened when he too noticed the girl, and he urged me forward.

"It's Bettina!" he exclaimed. "She must have been on the same flight that you came in on! We weren't expecting her home for another few days!"

"Hey, there, Bettina!" he called out gaily, distracting the girl's attention from Leo. "Don't tell me you got tired of watching all those fashion shows you were meaning to see in Florence!"

The young woman looked round, smiling, but seeing Jake's arm linked in mine, her smile seemed to waver, and a frown crossed her face.

"Are you here too, Jake!" she was smiling again. "How very nice of you and Leo to come and meet me, but as I was asking Leo, when you interrupted me, how on earth did you know what flight we would be arriving on?"

"We?" Jake looked surprised. "Do you mean to say you have all come back today?"

Bettina nodded, and the hooped gold earrings which dangled from the lobes of her tiny ears flashed like miniature lightnings as she did so.

"Sally could not stand the heat in the city another moment. She said Florence felt like a furnace, and she simply had to get back to the Villa Magnolia with its fresh sea breezes, or she would collapse. So," she shrugged, "since she is the boss when Richard is away, that meant we all had to pack and come home!"

As she was speaking, Bettina kept eyeing me surrepetitiously, obviously trying to hide her curiosity as to who I was, for the two men had been so surprised and pleased to see her, that they seemed to have forgotten about me, and had made no effort to introduce us to each other.

I gave Jake a sharp nudge.

"I am still here, you know!" I reminded him.

"I am sorry, Melissa," he turned to me apologetically. "I forgot for the moment that you did not

21

know Bettina—Bettina Morton, one of our new neighbours. Bettina, this is Melissa, Melissa Gilchrist, who as we told you before you departed for Florence, decided to come to and save us from Jane's cooking!"

The girl held out her hand and for a brief instant our fingers made contact as she said.

"So you are Melissa?" she seemed taken aback. "Somehow I had pictured you as being older. As a matter of fact," she blurted out, "you don't look old enough to be a fully qualified teacher!"

I shrugged. "It is amazing how casual clothes and a casual hair style can lop years from one's age, Miss Morton," I replied lightly, thinking that she too would look much more youthful if she looked less like a *Vogue* fashion plate.

"It is Mrs. Morton, not Miss," she corrected me, adding quickly, "but either makes me sound too fuddy duddy, so make it Bettina, please!"

As she was speaking a low, husky voice interrupted us.

"Leo! Jake!" There was a note of pleasure in the tone. "How nice to see you! Have you just come in from one of your surveys?"

Jake looked round, smiling, and I turned too, to look at the newcomer, as Bettina said quickly.

"They didn't come to meet us, if that is what you were thinking, Sally. They came to meet Melissa, here, who was on the same flight as we were!"

"Oh!" The tall, attractive looking blonde who had joined us looked at me with surprised eyes. "So you are Melissa? Somehow I thought—"

"That you would look older!" Leo and Jake finished for her, and everyone laughed as I held out my hand to her and said.

"Yes, I am Melissa Gilchrist."

"And I am Sally Devlin," she introduced herself before Jake could do so. "Your uncle's next door neighbor, as I expect you will have guessed.

Sally Devlin's fingers were hot and moist to touch, and as I looked at her face, I noticed that under her careful make-up, she showed signs of strain. For a moment I wondered if she was nervous of plane travel, as many people are, but if this was the case, then she would have been wiser to take the ferry boat from Genoa to Olbia, instead of enduring the discomfort of air travel.

"I do hope you will enjoy your stay in Alghero, Melissa," the smile she gave me as she released her grip of my hand was tremulous.

"I am sure I shall," I replied, more than ever convinced from her expression that she was not feeling well, or that something had happened in the past few minutes which had disturbed her.

"This is Dirk," Sally turned away from me to beckon to a small boy who was resentfully trying to pull his hand away from the restraining grip of a raven-haired young woman who had the face of a Rossetti Madonna.

He was a handsome lad of about eight or nine, with dark, brown curly hair, blue eyes and a rebellious mouth. I guessed that this was the lad my uncle had mentioned in his letter as my future pupil. I also surmised that he was no prissy little Lord Fauntleroy who would appreciate being babied by the women of his father's household, and

23

looking down into his bright, intelligent eyes, and noting the way he jutted out his chin at a defiant angle, I decided he might prove quite a handful.

"Hello, Dirk!" I ignored the unsmiling regard as I held out my hand to him. "I have been hearing about you from my uncle. He tells me that you are interested in things like lizards and beetles, so I asked one of my brothers to send me out a nature book which has just been published, to give to you. I am quite sure you will find it interesting."

The wariness faded from the young eyes, to be replaced by a flicker of interest.

"Do you know much about insects and things?" he demanded.

"I know a little," I replied, "but I am sure you will be able to teach me more," I released my hold of his hand.

"I know lots and lots about them!" he bragged, "and—"

"Just a minute, young man," interrupted Sally pleasantly. "You can chat about your insects at a later date, but in the meantime," she nudged him towards the Mercedes, "in you get! We want to get home before your father's phone call comes through!"

Dirk wriggled away from her guiding hand as she turned to me again to introduce me to the dark haired woman who was standing a foot or so away from us.

"This is Eve, Eve Yuille," she beckoned the girl forward. "Eve is an indispensable member of the Devlin household!" she said in a friendly tone. "Eve, I expect you have already gathered that this is Max's niece, Melissa."

I shook hands with the third young woman, while a uniformed chauffeur carefully piled the several suit cases the women had brought with them into the trunk, sullenly watched by Dirk who had not obeyed his mother's command to get into the car.

"Come on now, Dirk!" said Sally briskly. "In you get!"

He gave her a pleading look.

"Couldn't I go with Jake and Leo in their car?" he asked. "I don't like going in the Mercedes. I always feel sick in it."

"You can sit in the front with Mario. You will feel all right there."

"But I want to go on talking to her!" he looked at me. "I want to tell her about my pet lizard!"

"No, Dirk," Sally surprised me with her firmness. "You will do as I say. Now, get into the front seat beside Mario and don't waste any more time. You will have plenty of opportunities to talk to Miss Gilchrist later."

He obeyed her sulkily. The three women took their seats in the big car. The chauffeur got into the drivers seat, and in seconds the Mercedes moved smoothly away from the curbside, with Dirk staring straight ahead, chin stuck aggressively out and his soft lips pouting with displeasure because he hadn't got his own way; in a manner which reminded me so strongly of Jake in his early teens when he had crossed swords with authority, and lost, that my heart warmed to him.

For the first time since I had considered taking on the job as a part-time tutor for a small boy during my stay in Sardinia, I found myself enthusiastic about it.

Dealing with a strong young personality like Dirk would be an interesting challenge, and far more rewarding than the work I had been doing in Montreux.

As I gazed after the departing car, I found myself wondering about the boy's father. Max had not gone into details about the Devlin household in his letter, merely saying that his next door neighbors were pleasant and very well-to-do. I wished he had told me more, for there was an aura of glamor about the three women I had just met, and Sally Devlin's face was one I recognized, although I did not know in what context.

Then, too, the name Devlin itself had a familiar ring, although I could not place it for the moment. Not that it mattered who the Devlins were, I shrugged as I turned away from the departing Mercedes. It was their son I would be in contact with, not them, and as their son's tutor I would be a mere employee to them, never a friend.

All the same, I thought happily, as I followed Jake to his car, what with one thing and another this visit to Sardinia promised to be rather intriguing and exciting.

Fortunately I could not at that moment foresee just how full of intrigue and excitement, and danger too, my stay in Sardinia was going to be!

THREE

"Well, Melissa?" Jake said as we got into the car, while Leo remained standing, waving to the departing Mercedes. "What do you think of the 'Three Graces' as Max calls them?"

I hesitated for a fraction of a second before replying.

"They are all very lovely, very elegant, and they seem very pleasant," I shrugged. "All the same, I feel a bit sorry for young Dirk. He does not seem to me to be the type of boy who enjoys being smother loved by a trio of doting women!"

"I don't think that I would object!" said Leo, who had opened the rear passenger door and was slipping into the seat behind Jake. "In fact, I don't think I could think of anything pleasanter than to have three beauties like Bettina, Eve and Sally dancing attendance on me!" he laughed.

I shook my head, ignoring his light-hearted retort, and turned to Jake. "With all these women around, I can't imagine why his father wants a woman to tutor him. Surely there are some male students or teachers in Alghero who would be pleased to undertake the job?"

"I doubt if Devlin would like to have a strange young man added to his household, especially when he is away from home so much," said Jake drily. "He has a reputation of being very jealous and very possessive where his women folk are concerned."

"Are the three girls related to each other?" I asked curiously. "Max wasn't very illuminating about the household in his letter. He did not even say what Devlin himself did."

"Didn't you recognise the name?" Leo leaned towards me with a surprised look on his face.

"It seems familiar," I frowned, "but I can't think why."

"Richard Devlin, Sally's husband, is Devlin the film producer, director, actor, writer, multimillionaire business tycoon!" Leo informed me. "You must have heard of him!"

"Oh!" I gasped. "Is that who he is! Oh!" I repeated, "How exciting! I think he is an amazing man!"

"So do most women!" Jake sighed. "I was hoping that you would not join the fan club!"

I was silent for a few moments, thinking about my future employer, before I asked my original question again.

"You still haven't told me where the other two girls fit into the household. I gather Sally is his wife and Dirk's mother."

"His second wife, and Dirk's step-mother," interjected Leo. "She was a stewardess with the air line on which he commuted between Rome and London."

"Rumor has it," put in Jake, "that Devlin married her because she was so good at dealing with young Dirk on those trips. He felt the boy needed a strict mother figure instead of his two adoring slaves, Eve and Bettina. It also has it that Bettina, who is the late Mrs. Devlin's sister and whose husband was killed in the same road accident as her sister, was not at all pleased about the marriage, because she had an eye on Devlin herself!"

"That's nonsense!" Leo said explosively. "Bettina was very glad to have the worry of disciplining a spoiled boy taken away from her! If anyone was annoyed by the marriage, it was Eve." He relapsed into silence.

Jake's flickering wink at me in the driving mirror confirmed what I had guessed earlier—that Leo was very much attracted to the pretty redhead, and to distract him from Jake's teasing I said,

"Where does Eve fit in, Leo?"

"She has been Richard's secretary and general girl Friday for eight years," he told me. "In fact, since shortly after his first marriage. Eve is the one who oils the wheels of everyday life for him, keeping him right about appointments and deals with social occasions he should attend. I understand that after Mary's death she even took over the running of the household for him, and managed to cope with Dirk too. Everyone thought they would eventually marry, although there was never a hint that their relationship was more than a business one."

"I don't think a relationship like they had would have led to a happy marriage," said Jake, and "and from what Eve has let drop, I think she was relieved when he met Sally! She is more a career woman than the domestic type, and it isn't, in any case, as if she doesn't have plenty of men to dance

29

attendance on her when she wants them to. I believe there is a boy friend back home, and as a matter of fact," he grinned, "Max is a great admirer of hers!"

"Max is a wily old devil!" observed Leo with a laugh. "He makes up to Eve, so that she will type out his reports for him!"

"And Eve likes coming to type his reports, because it gives her an excuse to flirt with Carlo!" chuckled Jake.

I settled back happily in my seat, glancing out at the darkness of the passing landscape, but unable to make out anything except the dim reflection of my own smiling face in the car window, and feeling surprisingly content at having the relationships of the three women explained to me, for I had gathered from his tone that Jake was not particularly interested in any of the pretty women we had been discussing, and was apparently still footloose and fancy free as I was myself.

"You know," I remarked, turning around to Leo. "I think I am going to like being here!"

"You mean, you think you are going to like meeting the great Devlin in person?" he teased.

I shook my head. "I am going to like working with his son. I don't think he is going to be the easiest of pupils to deal with, but teaching him will be a change from working with girls who were more interested in clothes and make-up and themselves, than in learning languages, or studying subjects of interest. As a matter of fact, Jake," I laughed, "you will never believe it, but one of the most important subjects on the curriculum,

30

and one which I was expected to teach them, was called 'Etiquette and Savoir-Vivre'!"

"What on earth did that cover?" he turned to me with an interested grin.

"When I tell you that my girls came from Germany, Japan, Nigeria, Nicaragua, South America, India, China, the States—with a couple of British girls for good measure—countries which all have different cultures and different ways of doing things, you can guess at the difficulties I had with this particular class. You see," I explained, "what I had to teach them was how to eat an orange the correct way, how to peel an apple, or fork up spaghetti—"

"Melissa! You are joking!" interrupted Leo with disbelief.

I shook my head. "Far from it. There were scores of things like that I had to explain to them! I had to explain about who should sit next to who at table, orders of precedence, selecting the right wines to go with the right dishes, and most important, I had to teach them the art of dinner table conversation!"

"Melissa! You are trying to pull our legs!" This time it was Jake who interrupted me.

"I'm not. Truly I am not! Surely you knew," I smiled at them, "that during dinner certain subjects are definitely taboo—subjects like politics or economics or work!

"As Madame Chellah, the principal pointed out, after a hard day at the office men and women want light conversation, about holidays, not illnesses; about amusing scandals, not the daily grind; about films and plays—that sort of thing!"

"I can tell you something about dinner table conversations!" chuckled Jake. "At the Villa Gelsomino, unless you know something about archaeology and nuraghe and prehistoric men and Etruscans, you will be out in the cold as far as we are concerned!"

"You could always talk about lizards!" Leo consoled me. "We have a fair number here!"

"It was smart of you to tell Dirk you knew of his interest in such things," put in Jake. "You took a trick with him, but then I was quite sure you and he would get on together. A girl who has been brought up with three older brothers and their friends, soon learns how to deal with the opposite sex!"

"There is only one thing about Dirk's interest in insects I should warn you of," said Leo. "Don't encourage him to catch them and bring them into the house. Sally has a horror of creepy crawlies! She went quite hysterical the other evening when a moth which had singed its wings on the patio light, fell into her hair."

"I would have been hysterical myself!" I told him. "Lizards and the like I don't mind, but moths and flying beetles I abhor, so if you should hear a scream in the night, it won't mean that I am being attacked by a maniac, merely that some horrible night flying creature has invaded my room!"

"That's right!" grinned Jake. "I remember the time I had to rescue you from the attack of a poor old daddy-long-legs! What a state you got into when it started to fly round your head!"

We sped on through the darkness until we came

32

into a brightly lit small town whose main street and pavement cafés were crowded with people.

"This is Alghero itself," explained Leo. "Our villa is on the far side of the town, out on a promontory, cheek by jowl with the Devlins' much more imposing residence!"

A few minutes later, after passing a curious looking round tower, which was floodlit, and a broad, well illuminated esplanade, we turned right, off the main highway, and approached a gateway, which was barred by an intricately designed wrought iron gate.

"The Villa Gelsomino!" announced Jake dramatically, pressing on the car horn to announce our arrival.

FOUR

At the sound of the horn, a door opened and a beam of light came flooding down the driveway. Leo got out of the car to open the gate, and as Jake drove slowly up the path, the tall, broad figure of my uncle appeared on the top step of the narrow flight which led to the front door.

He came hurrying towards me as I alighted from the car.

"Melissa, my dear!" he gave me an affectionate hug. "You have no idea how pleased we all are to have you with us!" He took me by the arm and led me into the house while Jake and Leo followed with my luggage.

Max thoughtfully took me to my bedroom straight away so that I could have a quick wash and freshen myself up before being introduced to the other members of his group.

When I went downstairs a few minutes later, I was taken into the dining room, where I was introduced to each person in turn. First I met the two undergraduate students from Max's university— Mike Harrison and Stanley Roe, and standing between Jake and Leo there was a friend of theirs from their college days, Carlo Vittorio Roncardi, a native Sard, who had been primarily responsible for getting the expedition organized.

Carlo was about Jake's height, with very dark and curly hair, damson black eyes, and a mahogany tan. He charmed me with the gaiety of his smile as I felt sure he charmed every woman he met. When we were introduced, he held my hand caressingly for a moment longer than was necessary, and his eyes sparkled with a flirtative interest as he looked down at me, but his admiring glance and his flirtative manner did not annoy me as, hours earlier, at Milan airport, I had been annoyed when another dark and handsome stranger had made plain his interest in me.

As he was remarking that he hoped I would enjoy my visit to Sardinia, the remaining member of the team came in to the room. This was Jane, the brilliant academic who was quite hopeless when it came to cooking, and also, as it happened, Leo's sister, although this was something Max had not mentioned when he wrote to me. Perhaps he thought I was already aware of the fact.

Jane was quite unlike her younger brother in general appearance, being tall and dark and angular in face and form, where he was small and square built, with a crop of brownish-fair hair, like Jake's, but they both had the same pleasant smile and friendly manner, and in the first few moments of our meeting, I knew that I was going to like her as much as I liked Leo.

"We have all been looking forward to your visit, Melissa," she assured me warmly, "and it isn't just because you are going to make life easier for us by looking after us that I say so!"

I looked round the circle of smiling, friendly faces and sighed.

"You have no idea how good it is to be here, and to be able to speak and joke in my own language again! At the Château, except during my English class, everyone had to speak French all the time, and that rule even applied in the dormitories and sick bay!"

As I was speaking I was aware of a most appetizing smell wafting into the dining room, and when I wrinkled my nose in appreciation, Jane giggled and said.

"The meal tonight will taste as good as it smells, Melissa, because I did not cook it!"

"We wanted to make sure you would stay," chaffed Max, "so Carlo persuaded one of his cousins to come and cook for us tonight, and she has prepared a famous Sardinian dish in your honor! Roast suckling pig with rosemary and all the trimmings!"

The meal was every bit as good as it had promised to be, and while we ate and drank, Max told me about the work they were doing on the island.

"What I don't understand," I said, as, contrary to the teaching of the class on Etiquette and Savoir-Vivre which I had recently been imparting to my pupils I dunked pieces of crusty bread into the delicious gravy, "is where Jake and Leo fit into an archaeological team? I thought that you two were working for a construction firm in Italy?"

Jake enlightened me.

"We are having a kind of busman's holiday, Melissa. As you know, since our days with the University Air Squadron, we have both been very keen on aerial photography. Well, aerial photography comes in very useful when it comes to discovering the sites of old cities and encampments which have long been buried under sand or overgrown by vegetation.

"Our contract in Italy was running out, but in our spare time there we had done quite a bit of this type of aerial research, and so we decided to write a book about it. When we then heard that Max was coming out to Sardinia to do some work here, it was only natural that we should offer him our services, as we were so nearly on the spot, and that is how we all got together!"

The friendly voices droned on about their work and their newest and most interesting discoveries, and I felt myself grow sleepier and sleepier. Overwork during the past few months, sudden relaxation among friends, to say nothing of my overenjoyment of Rosa's cooking and the heady local Sardinian wines, were all combining to make me feel fuzzy minded, and I could scarcely keep my eyelids from drooping over my tired eyes.

Jane, who was seated opposite me, looked up and caught me trying to stifle a yawn.

"It's about time we let Melissa have a word in!" she said kindly. "She must be bored to tears with all our technical talk!"

I shook my head. "I am not the least bit bored. Max knows I have quite an interest in his work, but," I spoke ruefully, "I am rather tired. I had to get up at the crack of dawn, and I have had so many changes to get connections to get me from Montreux to here, that I am very weary!"

I pushed my chair back. "Please don't think me rude, but I must go off to bed now. If I wait any longer," I smiled, "someone will have to carry me upstairs!"

There were laughing offers from all the men present to do this, but I insisted that I did not want to break up the party. I made my way up to my bedroom, and the others carried their coffees and liqueurs out to the patio, where they could sit back in the garden chairs and enjoy the spicy warmth of the night air.

My bedroom was on the first floor, at the gable end of the villa, and overlooked the patio and the terraced garden which dipped by degrees to the high wall on the edge of the promontory on which the house was built. From this wall, according to Jake, the cliffs dropped almost sheerly down to a little sandy cove, where he often bathed in the early morning.

It was a largish, spacious room, with white painted walls, white painted furniture, and whitish goat skin rugs covering the tiled floor.

As I opened the bedroom door, the white net curtains screening the french windows, which were still ajar, billowed in toward me, like ghostly genie, and I recoiled, startled by the unexpected movement and the picture it had conjured up in my mind, before walking across the room to step out onto the little balcony festooned with twining branches of wistaria, whose fading flowers were now almost hidden by clusters of scented white jasmine which had intertwined with the other vine.

I stood for a moment looking out across the sea. From where I stood, I could see the winking beam of the lighthouse across the bay, and nearer, barely visible over a mass of trees, the side wall of a neighbouring house, which I assumed must be the Villa Magnolia.

A moth flew against my face and I retreated hastily into the bedroom. I undressed and took a quick shower before crawling sleepily between the cool, lavender scented sheets of a most comfortable bed.

Two kittens, who had attracted my admiring attention in the dining room earlier in the evening, had followed me up to my room, and as I settled down in bed they snuggled together, purring loudly in unison, on the skin rug beside the window.

I curled up into a cosy ball. As I drifted to sleep, I was vaguely aware of the rumble of voices which drifted through the open window from the patio below. I could detect Jake's deep guffaw at some remark that had been made, and Max's chuckle mingling with Jane's light laugh, and I thought how very pleasant it was to be among friends of my own again, as the waves of sleep gradually enveloped me.

It must have been several hours later that the pained and frightened yowl from one of the kittens jerked me back to full consciousness.

I sat upright in bed, clutching the sheet round me as I shivered with cold at the sudden awakening.

I stared in the direction of the sound and saw, silhouetted against the moonlight which streamed across the balcony and through the open window of my room, the dark shape of a man who was coming towards me, hands outstretched.

For a moment I was too petrified to move, or even scream, but when I saw the scarf held between his hands, saw the frightfulness of his leering face distorted out of recognition behind a nylon stocking mask, my senses returned. I rolled to the other side of the bed, away from the menacing hands, and screamed with the full strength of my lungs.

My scream, like a long drawn out, belated echo of the kitten's earlier yowl when the intruder had stepped on her as he came through the window, brought anxious shouts from the rooms on either side of the passageway, and immediately my assailant turned and rushed back on to the balcony, to clamber, like an agile gorilla, over the iron rail and drop from sight.

FIVE

"Melissa! What is wrong? What is going on here?"
Max came rushing into the room.

"There—there was a man here!" I gasped. "He
was coming toward the bed. He pounced towards
me and I thought he was going to strangle me!" I
gave a convulsive shudder.

Jake, tousle-headed, incongruous looking in a
short kimono-type dressing gown, appeared in the
doorway.

"What is wrong, Melissa?" he repeated Max's
question, then added, after looking around the
room and seeing no cause for alarm. "Don't tell
me all that fuss was over one of your night flying
beetles!"

"Of course it wasn't!" I said indignantly.
"Someone came into my room, over the balcony.
He disturbed the kittens who were asleep on the
rug over there. They yowled and woke me as he
rushed towards me. I screamed and rolled away
from him, and when you both shouted back he
turned and darted back over the balcony!"

Jake crossed to the french window and peered
down into the garden, but he could see no move-
ments among the deep shadows of the bushes, and
with a shake of his head he came over to me and
sat on the edge of my bed.

"It's all right, Melissa," he took my hand in a comforting clasp. "There is no one there. Don't you think," he added with a wry smile, "that Rosa's savoury roast pig and Carlo's strong Sardinian wine combined to give you a nightmare?"

I withdrew my hand from his and said angrily. "It was no nightmare, Jake!" I shuddered. "There was someone in my room!"

I was feeling cold and shivery with reaction, and I hugged the sheet tightly round me. Jane, who had by this time also arrived, pushed Jake aside and put a friendly arm round my shoulders.

"Nightmare or no nightmare," she rounded on the men, "Melissa has had a fright. So Jake," she ordered, "off you go and fetch her a brandy. If it does nothing else, at least it will warm her up a bit. She is as cold as ice!"

"Jane, there was someone in my room," I persisted. "It wasn't a nightmare!"

"No, it wasn't!" said Max slowly, as he came back into the room from the balcony where he had remained peering all around him. "Look at this!" He held out a torn branch of wistaria. "And apart from this broken limb, there is a trail of bruised and broken leaves along the railing, and below the balcony, the trellising had been torn from the wall when your intruder made his hurried getaway!"

I gasped again and Jane held me more closely. Jake, returning with the brandy in time to hear the tail end of what Max had said, thrust the bottle and glass to Jane, and went striding back to the balcony to examine the damage for himself.

"Sorry, Melissa," he apologized, grim faced. "If

I still hadn't been half asleep when I looked out the last time, I would have spotted the damage myself, and I might even have seen the fellow and had a chance to go after him!"

"Then it is as well that you didn't notice the torn plants," said Jane sharply. "You don't know what sort of weapons the young layabout was carrying, and you might have been very badly hurt!" Her face went white as she turned to Max.

"Don't you think it is time you telephoned the police?" she looked worried. "He might still be lurking in the garden for all we know!"

"Nonsense!" said Max. "He will be miles away by now! A blackguard like that is not going to hang around to be caught by the police when they arrive!"

"Do you think we have to go to all the fuss to get in touch with the police?" he asked. "There is not very much they can do except go trampling all over the place and ask a lot of questions which we won't be able to answer helpfully. It isn't as if anything was stolen," he went on.

"Melissa got an awful fright!" said Jane.

"But she wasn't hurt," put in Leo. "No, I am inclined to agree with Jake. If we bring in the police, there will be questions, questions, questions and lots of red tape to wrap them up in, and we shall not get any peace to get on with our work."

"I am inclined to agree with you both," said Max thoughtfully, "but there is something I think we should do, which will keep us on the right side of the law, so to speak, without causing us undue bother." He glanced at Jake. "Why not get in

45

touch with Carlo and tell him what has happened."

"Carlo?" I exclaimed. "Where does he come into this?"

"Carlo's brother-in-law is the Captain of Police," Jane explained, nodding her head with approval at Max's suggestion. "And now that we have settled what is to be done, I shall go downstairs and make a nice cup of tea to calm us all down before we go back to bed."

"I'll make the tea for you!" Jake offered with alacrity.

"Count me out for a cup," I said, yawning. "That more than generous glass of brandy Jane poured for me is already making my head spin, and I am sure I shall be out for the count before you even get to the kitchen, Jake!"

"Are you quite sure?" asked Jane.

I nodded and settled back with my head on the pillow and the sheet drawn snugly up to my chin.

"Wouldn't you like me to stay in your room for the night," she suggested. "Jake and Leo could easily carry my bed in here."

"No, thanks," I murmured drowsily. "I have got over my fright, and I am quite sure that the man won't dare come back again tonight. They say," I murmured hazily, "that lightning never strikes twice in the same place," I gave a silly giggle.

"It wasn't a laughing matter!" said Jake angrily. "Moreover, you have only yourself to blame for the incident!" he added as he strode across to the window, and slammed the wooden shutters in place, pushing the hasp firmly into position. "In

46

this part of the world, you are inviting trouble by leaving both your windows and your shutters wide open! I thought you would have learned a little common sense by now!" he snapped.

"Come off it, Jake!" Jane reprimanded him for his brusque tone. "There is no need to scold Melissa like that! The villa is so far from the main road that even I have never considered closing the shutters or the window when I go to bed!"

"Then you ought to, Jane!" retorted Jake, his voice still harsh. "I could expect Melissa to be scatter-brained, but I have always given you credit for good sense!"

Jane made a face at him. "Away with you, Jake!" she laughed. "You are just talking to get out of making this pot of tea you so rashly promised us!"

Max chuckled as he urged the others out of the room ahead of him. "That's right, Jane," he said. "It is high time someone tried to keep that godson of mine in order!"

He turned back to smile at me. "Goodnight, Melissa. If you do feel at all nervous, give a bang on the wall. My bedroom is right next door, and I am a light sleeper."

The others said goodnight, and when the door had closed behind them, I snuggled down into the bed. The kittens came padding out from under the bed and jumped lightly up beside my feet, where they made themselves comfortable, and I fell asleep to the contented rumble of their purrs.

Hours later I was wakened by the clattering of dishes, the murmur of voices from the patio, the scraping rasp of chairs being dragged across the concrete flags, and the joyful boom of Max's laugh.

Lazily I rolled over and yawned and stretched, and two furry bundles darted at my fingers and tried to chew them, waking me most effectively from my somnolent state!

I slithered from bed, and wrapping my robe around me, crossed over to open the shutters and step out on the balcony. Below me, on the patio, Jane was setting dishes out on the long trellis table which had been carried from the dining room. She looked up as I called "Good morning!"

"Hi, there!" she greeted me. "You have had a nice long sleep in spite of what happened! How do you feel?"

"Lazy!" I laughed.

"Breakfast is in five minutes," she told me. "The coffee is perking."

"And even Jane can't go wrong there!" My uncle came up the steps from the shrubbery and waved to me. "Jake and Leo have gone off to fetch fresh rolls from the local bakery, so you have nothing to fear there either!"

Jane took the teasing about her culinary abilities in good part, saying cheerfully, "Like you Max, I can't be good at everything, and at least," she chaffed him, "I don't need to use my fingers to count!"

I dressed quickly, putting on a pair of well cut denims and a blouse which matched the blue of my eyes. I brushed my shoulder length hair and tied it back tidily with a fine blue chiffon scarf, before hurrying downstairs to join the others.

"I feel a bit guilty," I said to Jane as I took my place at table. "Preparing breakfast is supposed to be my duty now."

"Not today. Not until Monday," she shook her head. "You must at least have a week-end break before you start work. In any case," she added practically, "I shall have to show you where things are kept, and tell you about the shopping and what not—so just relax!" she smiled and poured me out a cup of coffee.

"Where are the others?" I asked.

"The youngsters, that is to say, Mike and Stan, have gone to spend the weekend with friends. Leo and Jake aren't back from the baker's as yet. I daresay they have bumped into friends and have forgotten the time, and Max is phoning Carlo to tell him about last night."

As she was speaking, Max came out of the house followed by Leo and Jake. I stood up to give my uncle a good morning peck on the cheek and he squeezed my waist affectionately before going to take his place at the head of the table.

I sat down again and was about to help myself to a roll from the basket, Jake was putting down on the table, but he moved it out of reach, saying, with a laugh.

"Oh, no, Melissa! You don't deserve one, showing such blantant favouritism to Max! Where is my good morning kiss?" he twinkled.

"We are not kissing kin!" I reminded him demurely as I made a sudden grab at the basket and seized a crisp round roll from it.

Jake looked at me, eyebrows raised, and said in a surprised voice. "No, we aren't, are we?" he shook his head. "And yet I always think of you as a member of my family. I suppose it is because we have known each other for so long!

"Do you know, Jane," he turned to the other girl with a mischievous grin on his face. "The first time I met Melissa, she was three or four, and being administered a spanking because she had climbed over an allegedly child-proof gate, to find out what went on in the road which ran past the house. Then—"

Fortunately he could not proceed with his teasing reminiscenes, because he was interrupted by the unexpected arrival of Carlo, who kissed first Jane's hand, and then mine, with a flourish, and a twinkle in his humorous eyes, before greeting the men and sitting down on the vacant chair beside me.

"I thought I should like to hear the story you told me over the telephone first hand from Melissa before getting in touch with my brother-in-law," he said to Max, turning his attention to me.

"I hope you will not hold what happened last night against my island," he smiled ruefully. "Most of the trouble here in Alghero during the summer months is caused by young holiday hoodlums from the mainland, who spend more than they can afford, and then try to find extra money for themselves by bag snatching and night prowling."

He ladled a heaping teaspoonful of sugar into the cup of coffee Jane had placed before him as he listened to my account of the incident.

"So there was no real harm done," he concluded. "Good. I can understand why you do not want to report the matter officially, for no one wants to get strangled in red tape unnecessarily, but I shall mention the matter to Patrizio unofficially, and tell him that since the Devlins are back in residence, he should assign an extra patrol car to the area. That will take care of the Villa Gelsomino as well as the Villa Magnolia, and no one will ask questions! After all," he concluded, "we do not want Melissa to have another such fright, do we?" he smiled at me and I could not help smiling back.

Carlo was very attractive. He had a pleasant face and a pleasant manner and the gayest, most twinkling eyes I had seen in a man. I could imagine he enjoyed life, and that a girl would enjoy going out and about with him, provided she did not take him too seriously!

"Do you think your brother-in-law will be able to send an extra patrol car here?" queried Max. "After last week's kidnapping, his resources must be stretched to the limit."

"That affair?" Carlo shrugged. "That was a purely local business and quickly dealt with. Indeed," he continued, "most of the kidnappings the international press make a to-do about from time to time as happening here, are purely local affairs, usually some poor shepherd trying to get hold of the rich landowner who is demanding too much rent from him, or even more personal affairs—family vendettas. The Sards rarely interfere with tourists or foreigners."

Are there still bandits operating in Sardinia?"

Carlo laughed.

"Si, Melissa. There are bandits still in Sardinia,

but then," he flashed me an amused smile, "there are bandits in every country, vero? I have heard that it is no longer safe for a man or a woman to walk alone in the streets of any of the major cities of the world, at nights.

"But our bandits are different," he went on. "For the most part they stay in the mountains of Barbagia, preying on their own kind and not on outsiders."

"I have read about Barbagia. I should like to visit the region."

Jake entered the conversation.

"If you want to learn anything about Sardinia, and particularly the region round Alghero, Carlo is your man, Melissa. He seems to know every inch of the countryside, and about its past history."

"And the loveliest beauty spots which the tourist board hasn't discovered and spoiled!" added Max.

"That reminds me," Carlo turned to Jane, holding out his cup for a refill of coffee. "The other reason I called this morning was to ask if you would all like to come on a picnic with my sister and her family tomorrow. We thought of spending the day at Lake Baratz."

"You hadn't anything planned for tomorrow, had you Jane?" asked Max.

She shook her head. "No, not for tomorrow."

"Then that is settled," Carlo stood up, and smiled at Jane. "My sister will provide the food. We shall leave you to take care of the wine and coffee!"

"Until tomorrow then," he looked at us, but his gaze lingered longest on my face. "Ciào!"

Max followed him to the front door, and Jake, seeing the smiling expression on my face laughed and said with a mock sigh, "Not you too, Melissa! Carlo steals all my girl friends!"

I grinned. "That's because you don't have his 'je ne sais quoi'!"

SIX

After breakfast, Jane decided to take me into Alghero so that she could show me the places where she usually shopped for food and other household supplies.

Jake and Leo were tinkering about under the hood of Max's elderly Rover, which he had brought out from England, and as we walked past them, Jake called out that he would meet us at the usual time at the usual café in town.

It was a pleasant walk from the villa, along the coast road to Alghero. On our right, set back from the road behind tamarisk hedges, were attractive-looking white villas, interspersed with an occasional tall, modern hotel. On our left was the sea, with its incredible range of colors, from lettuce green where it lapped the shore stretching through every conceivable shade of blue to the misty lilac of the horizon, where it merged with the cloudless Mediterranean sky.

As we walked along, we ran the gamut of wolf whistles, candidly admiring remarks and snatches of soulful serenades from the workers on the building sites of the new hotels which were being erected; from youthful Romeos who buzzed past us on their Vespas, almost falling off their little motor scooters as they turned to ogle us; and from strolling "pappagalli," the hopeful Casanovas who parade the streets of most Italian towns, pestering women whether they are accompanied or not, with their unwanted attentions.

Fortunately, because I found their impertinent remarks somewhat disconcerting, by the time we reached the more crowded Lungomare Dante, they found other women to devote their remarks to, although from behind me I could still hear the occasional loudly spoken "Bella! Bella!" or "È molto simpatica!" from admiring males.

"I call this walk into town 'running the gauntlet'!" Jane dismissed the ordeal lightly. "It is quite surprising, though, how soon you get used to it. Half the time the lads merely utter the phrases because they feel it is expected of them, but if you ignore them, they accept it, and turn their attentions to more gullible females!"

We walked past crowded pavement cafés and through a network of narrow roads which radiated out from a square overlooked by a round tower, where swallows dived and chased one another and squeaked their shrill high-pitched noises.

Many of the shops we passed were dark caverns, below the level of the road. I noticed a number of fascinating boutiques and junk shops, but we were not window or dress shopping on this occasion, and Jane did not give me a chance to peer into them as she hurried me along another broader street, and through an entrance in a high wall which stretched half the length of the avenue, to the local open air fruit and vegetable market.

I had thought the fruit market in Montreux colorful, but it did not compare with its Alghero counterpart. Never had I seen so many stalls of fruit as here! Pyramids of luscious, downy-cheeked peaches contrasted with piles of plum-colored aubergines; sun-kissed apricots offset the deep crimson of baskets of cherries, and potatoes and carrots, celery and asparagus, beans and artichokes were set out on the trestle tables, looking so fresh and clean and mouth watering that I was tempted to buy everything I saw, but Jane poked and examined everything with care before she bought the items on her shopping list.

I bemoaned the fact that I had not brought my camera with me. "I should love to photograph all this," I waved my hand, thus attracting the attention of the stall owner, who mistook my gesture and handed me the magnificent peach I had inadvertently pointed to.

"Due, por favore!" I smiled at her, buying a second peach to hand to Jane, and giggling like a couple of schoolgirls, we sunk our teeth into the luscious fruit.

"Isn't it gorgeous!" I turned to Jane as the sun-warmed juice trickled down my chin. "If only my ex-pupils could see me now, they would wonder how I had the nerve to teach them about etiquette!"

As I was speaking to her, I noticed a man withdraw hastily behind a nearby stall. There was no reason for me to think that he was any different from any of the dozens of other men who had been leering at us this morning, and yet I could have sworn that I had seen this particular pappagallo hanging about at the junction where the road from our villa met the main road, and again, mingling with a group of other men, following us along the esplanade.

"Come on, Melissa," Jane wiped her mouth to remove the last traces of peach juice. "I still have to take you to the fish market. Max and Jake love sea food dishes."

She led me across a narrow lane into an area similar to the one we had left, but here it was the fruit of the sea which piled the counters. There were large lobsters and bunches of mussels, and although the red mullet and tuna fish looked tempting, I did not fancy the eels and octopuses!

Max, Jake and Leo had all joked to me about Jane's cooking and domestic abilities, saying that although she was a brilliant scholar and an up-and-coming name in the field of archaeology, her housewifely talents were nil, but one thing they had not appreciated was her ability to judge the quality and freshness of the food she bought for them, for she knew exactly what points to look for when buying meat and fish, poultry and vegetables, and what was every bit as important, she knew how to drive a hard bargain with the stall keepers!

In the hours we spent shopping for the household I learned a great deal from her, and when we were leaving the market, I told her so.

"Shopping is the one domestic chore at which I am any good!" she smiled. "As you have heard, my attempts at cookery are invariably disastrous, and when it comes to mending and sewing the results are even worse!

"Jake teases me by saying that my idea of darn-

58

ing is even more primitive than his, since I merely draw the edges of the holes together, to the discomfort of everyone's feet, and," she shrugged ruefully, "they even stopped letting me do the household washing after I put all the clothes into the machine together, set it for boiling, and the sheets and the underwear and their best shirts came out a streaky orange shade from contact with my favourite nightie!"

"Oh no! Oh, Jane! Poor you!" I tried to comfort her. "Anyone can make a mistake like that!"

"Yes, I suppose so, but most people only make it once!" she grinned shamefacedly. "You see, the time before that I dyed everything blue, when I stuck Jake's new cords in with the other things, and before that I machine-washed woollies in spite of the 'hand wash only' label, and they shrunk so much we had to give them to Rosa's children!" she sighed again before adding with a twinkle.

"Never mind! At least by now my future husband has an idea what he is letting himself in for, so he won't be disillusioned!"

I shot her a surprised look. "Jane! I did not know that you were engaged!" I glanced at her hands, but her fingers were ringless.

She blushed. "It's not official, Melissa. I didn't mean to say anything to anyone just yet, because we want to keep quiet about our romance in the meantime." She flushed a deep pink. "So please, Melissa," she pleaded, "don't tell anyone what I have told you, especially Leo!" She bit her lip. "You know what a tease my brother can be, and this is something I could not bear to be teased about. It means too much to me," she ended fiercely, and abruptly turned away from me, and headed for the market exit, leaving me to follow her in a stunned silence after the surprising but unintentional disclosure.

Jane Hunter was in love! Jane Hunter was going to get married! It was obvious from her remarks that her future husband was one of the men she was working with, and since Mike and Stan were at least ten years younger than she was, although she had named no names, there was no doubt at all who she meant. It must be Jake!

Jake? I frowned. I could not imagine Jake in love with anyone. I could not imagine Jake married. Yet the more I considered Jane's words, the more obvious the answer became.

She and Jake had been students together at the university. Jake was her brother's best friend, and I knew that the trio had, during their college vacations, toured the continent together.

I liked Jane. I liked Jake. They would make a good marriage, of that I felt sure. I should have felt pleased for both of them, and yet I could not summon up any enthusiasm for the romance.

I wondered if Max had guessed at the position, and what he thought about it. Feeling strangely discontented and on edge, I followed Jane down the street which led into the older part of the town, where she had still more shopping to do.

As we walked along over the sunless cobbles of the Via Principe Umberto, where a gaudy array of washing swung in lines stretched out over the narrow street, I found it difficult to believe that we were now passing through the main street of the old town.

We had to go in single file at times, and keep close to the walls of the buildings to let motor traffic pass by. When we veered left into another equally narrow thoroughfare, I turned to Jane to say that I thought it a pity that two of Alghero's most important buildings, the Cathedral of Santa Maria and the Doria Palace should be so hemmed in by other buildings so that it was impossible to stand back and admire them.

As I looked toward her, over her shoulder, about fifteen yards further up the street, I saw the man I had already seen in the fruit market. He stopped abruptly and stood looking into one of the shop windows. His presence made me feel uneasy, and I said to Jane.

"There is a man tagging behind us. He has followed us all the way from the villa, or at least," I decided to give him the benefit of the doubt, "I am almost sure that it is the same man!"

Jane laughed. "These pappagalli all look the same, Melissa. The thing to do," she advised me, "is to pretend you haven't noticed him, so don't look round again, and he will soon lose interest!"

I tried to take her advice, but every now and then, when I stopped to admire a display of coral, or leather work, or cork postcards in the many little shops along our route, I would look covertly in the reflection of the street given by the window glass, and still following us, although at a most discreet distance, I could see the mirrored reflection of my admirer.

His persistence was beginning to annoy me, and I felt like challenging him directly and telling him that I would complain to the police, when he actually came in to the record shop in the Via Carlo Alberto, where Jane was wanting to have a look through the albums, for a birthday present!

"The man has followed us in here!" I started to tell her, when the assistant interrupted me, to tell Jane she had switched on the record she wanted to hear.

It was a record of the greart opera choruses of Verdi, by the Choir and Orchestra of La Scala, Milan, conducted by Claudio Abbato, and Jane listened to it with rapt attention. I listened to it as well, forgetting about my pest in the beauty of the music.

I decided that I would like to buy this recording as well, but unfortunately there was only one in stock. The assistant offered to telephone to their branch in Sassari to find out if she could get one from there for me, and while she waited to be put through, Jane kept glancing impatiently at her watch.

"I hope she will be quick!" she said. "I had not realized how late it was. Jake and Leo will be waiting for us at the Ciào Ciào!"

After some minutes the assistant came back, and informed me that there was a record at their branch in Sassari, and that it would be sent to Alghero for me.

"You will be able to collect it here on Monday afternoon," she told me.

"Thank you very much for your trouble!" I smiled gratefully, while she carefully slipped the records Jane had bought into a black and white plastic bag.

"Prego!" she replied courteously, and held the door of the shop open for us.

I stood for a moment and looked up and down the street to see if I could see my admirer, for he had left the shop after buying a record for himself, while we had been listening to the Orchestra of La Scala.

To my relief, he was nowhere to be seen, and feeling more light-hearted, I followed Jane back up the narrow, cobbled street, stopping, as the occasion demanded, to press close to the shops to let a car pass.

"Thank goodness it is a one way street," said Jane crossly, "or we might have been held up longer! Even as it is, I wonder what Jake and Leo are saying about us!" She caught my arm and hurried me into another equally narrow street at right angles to the one we had left.

At this moment, a big, powerful motor bicycle came zooming down the Via Gilbert Ferret.

"He is going much too fast!" snapped Jane angrily, as an elderly woman ahead of us turned to shake her fist at the driver, who had almost knocked her down as she stepped from the doorway of the dress shop on the corner.

The words were hardly out of her mouth when the motorbike swerved in our direction, as though it had skidded on the damp cobbles. The driver did not seem able to control it, and when it was only a couple of yards away from us, he panicked and jumped, leaving the mechanical monster to come slithering right at us with increasing speed.

The old woman screamed. A man on the other side of the road let out a shout of warning, but we were both aware of our own danger, and flung ourselves without further ado into the shelter of a shop doorway.

The machine crashed into the wall only a couple of feet away from us, the handle-bars and front wheel buckling under the impact, sending plaster and brickwork spraying in every direction, shattering the shop window, and spattering the street with broken glass.

In seconds the alley was crowded with babbling, excited shoppers, rushing to find out what had happened.

"Where is the driver?" cried the old woman. "He should be arrested! He was a madman!" She gesticulated wildly, making a drama of her own part in the affair. "He tried to kill me!"

The driver, however, had made himself scarce, and we decided to follow his example. We did not want to be detained as witnesses by the stout policeman who came puffing down the alley to see what was happening, and slipped out of sight round the corner.

"This way," Jane grabbed my arm and pushed me back the way we had come, until we arrived at another narrow street, which eventually led us to the Piazza Sulis, and the open air café, where Jake and Leo had arranged to meet us.

SEVEN

We hurried round the corner into the Piazza Sulis, and I spotted Leo and Jake seated at one of the round tables on the perimeter of the open air café, in the shade of a large, striped sunshade.

Although Jake was facing in our direction, he had not noticed us as yet. He was sitting sideways to the table, and I could see his fingers beating an impatient tattoo on the polished top, and a scowl of resentment at being kept waiting for so long, marred the usual pleasant expression of his face.

It was an attitude I remembered well from the past, as I still remembered so many things about Jake—his moods—his expressions—the pleasure I felt when I heard his voice or his laugh—and a wave of tenderness swept over me, because in the years between our meeting again, he had not changed. He was still the Jake who had been my good friend, my helper-out-of-scrapes; the Jake whom I had laughingly proposed to one Leap Year's day, when I was fourteen, and filled with jealousy which I tried to hide, for the girl he had brought home for his college mid-term holiday, to be his partner at one of my brothers' coming-of-age parties.

At this moment I could remember with amazing clarity the amused expression on his face when I had made the offer, and his mock serious acceptance of it.

"Of course I shall marry you, Melissa," he had promised. "But you will have to grow up first! Marriage is not a legal contract at fourteen!"

Somewhere in my old desk at home, among a hotch potch of other sentimental mementoes was the tiny gilt ring with the red stone from the birthday cracker which we had pulled together, and which he had laughingly slipped on my ring finger.

This particular memory brought the blood coursing warmly to my cheeks, staining them a deeper color than my newly acquired sun flush, and it was at this moment I knew why I had been so keen to come to Sardinia, why I had never been able to fall deeply in love with any of the young men who had drifted in and out of my life. Subconsciously, consciously now, I knew I had compared them all with Jake, and found them wanting. For me, Jake was the ideal man, the man I could laugh with and cry with and love, yes love! Yes, I realized with a feeling of panic, lest my face betray my thoughts, I had always been in love with Leo, from the days of hero-worshipping childhood, through jealous adolescence, and the years when, although we had rarely seen each other, I had thought of him at odd times of the day, thinking what fun it would have been to share this or that experience with him.

I wanted to turn and run. I wanted to have time to pull myself together before I faced him, but Jane was behind me, nudging me forward, nodding at me to sit down in the vacant seat at the far side of the table as she smiled down at Jake and said apologetically, "I am so sorry we are late, but—"

"Well?" Jake interrupted her with an air of feigned resignation. "What is your excuse this time?" he asked, as if being kept waiting by Jane was something he had come to expect.

"It is one you will find hard to believe," she chuckled, placing her shopping basket on the table, and slipping into the other vacant chair. "We have been dodging the police!"

"You have been what?" exclaimed Leo, looking from Jane to me with disbelief.

"Dodging the police! Keeping out of trouble!" she said, but I detected a tremor in her voice, which told me that she was only now beginning to appreciate what might have happened to us.

"What do you mean?" Jake frowned.

"If both Melissa and I had not been equally quick thinking and equally agile, you might have had to wait a very long time for us to come here!" she was doing her best to make light of what had happened.

"Come! Explain what you are getting at, Jane!" Leo said sharply.

Jane looked across the table at me.

"I am beginning to think that Melissa attracts trouble!" she shook her head. "The fact is, only minutes ago, we were both nearly knocked down in the Via Gilbert Ferret, by one of the local Hell's Angels!"

"You were what?" ejaculated Jake harshly, as he glanced with a frown from Jane to me.

In spite of the deep golden tan which I had admired yesterday, the skin of his cheeks seemed to have paled and tightened over his cheek bones, and the vein at his left temple throbbed visibly, a certain sign that he was upset.

His eyes were fixed steadfastly on Jane's face as she told him what had taken place, and as I watched them, the euphoria I had experienced only seconds earlier evaporated.

It wasn't Jane's clear description of the incident, reminding me again how narrowly she and I had missed being killed, or at very least, badly injured by the skidding motor bicycle, which made me feel cold and sick, with a desire to burst into tears. It was Jake's reaction as he listened to her tale.

He gripped the chrome arms of the chair in which he was sitting so tightly that I thought his knuckle bones would break through the skin. It was almost as if by gripping something to the breaking point he was able to control some deeper, inner emotion from showing, an emotion, which I was convinced had something to do with the girl at whose face he was staring with such concentration.

Looking at them both, seeing the expression on Jake's face, remembering what Jane had told me earlier, I had to face the fact that my dream of love was over, for it was not until I had seen the expression on Jake's face at this moment, that the reality of the romance she had told me about was brought home to me.

"Didn't the policeman whistle for you to come back, when he saw you taking off?" asked Leo.

"Why should he?" Jane shrugged. "There were plenty of other witnesses who were all too eager to tell him what had happened, without our getting involved."

"In any case," I put in. "We would not have been of much help. We were too busy jumping for our lives to notice in which direction the man ran, and before the bike skidded toward us, we were not paying a lot of attention to the driver, to notice what he looked like, at least," I turned to Jane, "I did not get a good look at him, did you?"

She shook her head. "He was just a bulky figure with a dark jacket, a white crash helmet and goggles," she shuddered. "Let's not talk about it any more. I don't want to even think of what might have happened if we hadn't been quick off our marks!"

I nodded in agreement. "It was a terrifying experience, and what I feel the need of right now is a cup of very strong, black coffee!"

"Me too!" agreed Jane.

The men ordered coffees, and after a few minutes, sitting there in the pleasant café, sipping our drinks in a leisurely fashion, watching the holiday-makers of many nationalities pass by, I forced myself to talk about my first impressions of Alghero, for by talking, I could force from my mind my disturbing thoughts of Jake and Jane, although every now and then I found myself giving them surreptitious looks, as though I hoped to catch them as they exchanged private glances of love, but apart from the look of strain and the tension he had evinced as he listened to Jane's earlier recital, neither by word nor glance did Jake give a further indication that Leo's sister was someone very special as far as he was concerned.

It was the same with Jane. Her manner toward my uncle's god-son was much the same as her manner toward her younger brother—a casually affectionate manner which betrayed nothing more than that they had been on friendly terms for a long time. There were no secret looks, no moments when hand deliberately brushed against hand for the pleasure of the physical contact with a loved one; no time when fingers twined momentarily with fingers in a loving caress.

I had finished my coffee, and Jake was trying to persuade me to sample one of the ice-cream concoctions which are a speciality of the Ciào Ciào, when Jane let out an exclamation of dismay.

"It is almost twelve o'clock!" she gasped. "I hadn't realized it was so late!" She hastily picked up her shopping basket from the table. "Oh, dear!" she bit her lip.

"What is the hurry, Jane?" asked Leo. "Have you forgotten that, thanks to Melissa, we have been granted a few day's break?"

"Of course I remembered we were on holiday," said Leo. "That is why I have already booked a table for four at your favorite sea-food restaurant. We thought it would be a pleasant change from your cooking!" he added, winking at me as he was speaking.

"You will have to cancel the reservation," said Jane crisply, pushing back her chair and standing up. "We have all been invited to the Devlin villa today, for a pre-lunch swim, and a luncheon to follow!"

"This is the first I have heard about that!" grumbled Leo.

Jane had the grace to blush. "That is because I forgot to tell you about it," she confessed. "Sally telephoned this morning, when you were out fetching the rolls, but what with one thing and another, and Carlo's unexpected appearance at breakfast, her invitation, which I had accepted for all of us, slipped my mind until this very moment!"

"It is as well we decided to come into town by car," Jake stood up and signalled the waitress to bring the bill. "We shall give you and Melissa a lift back home, so that you will have a little time to pretty yourselves to compete with the glamor pusses next door!"

Jane laughed. "Joke!" she grimaced. "We could never come up to their standard of glamor! In any case," she gave a sly dig at her brother, "you wouldn't like us to outshine your Bettina, would you?"

"I wish she was my Bettina," Leo heaved a sigh, "but I don't think I am her type. To begin with," he pointed out, "I have no money. Could any of you picture a doll like that chasing round the globe with an underpaid geologist?"

"She might enjoy the change from riches to rags," Jake encouraged him, "you never can tell with a woman!"

"That is true!" said Leo optimistically, and hurried off to cancel the reservation he had made, while Jake handed the waitress some notes, told her to keep the change, and led us to the far end of the square, where his car was parked.

When we arrived back at the Villa Gelsomino, Max was pottering about in the back garden, trying to tie back into position the trellis work which the intruder had torn down in his flight the previous evening.

"Come on, Max!" Jane ordered him. "It's time to trim your beard and tidy yourself before lunch!" she glanced at his baggy trousers and the tattered espadrilles he was wearing.

"Melissa, you don't object to the way I look, do you?" he appealed to me hopefully.

"Melissa may not," intervened Jane, "but your Three Graces would not be at all impressed if they saw you looking as you do now!"

"What do you mean?"

"We are lunching at the Villa Magnolia today," she told him. "After all the cracks you have been making about my meals, I did not think you would object to my accepting an invitation to eat elsewhere!" she twinkled at him.

"Dear Jane," he said affectionately, "your cooking isn't as bad as we make out!"

Jane laughed. "Max, you would say anything for an excuse not to have to get dressed up! Honestly!" she shook her head, "I hate to think of some of the odd rig outs in which you appeared in public, before I took you in hand and made an effort to keep you in order!"

"And they talk about equality for women!" sighed Max. "I think it is high time we men stood up for ourselves for a change!"

He rubbed his fingers over his curling beard. "Jane, do I need to go to the Devlins today?" he asked pleadingly.

She nodded. "I have accepted for you, and Max,

72

you know that once you get there, you always enjoy yourself."

"When Richard is there, yes, but today it will only be his women folk."

"Never mind, we shall be there to support you, Max!" Jake reminded him.

"What is more, we shall be able to have a swim in their pool before lunch," put in Leo with enthusiasm. "That will save us the clamber down the steep path from our garden to the cove for our usual swim."

"It isn't the climb down so much as the climb back that I object to!" drawled Jake. "I think we ought to do a repair job on that path before it becomes definitely dangerous."

Jane moved across to the kitchen entrance with her basket of groceries, but turned, as she reached the door to add, as an afterthought.

"By the way, when I spoke to Sally on the phone this morning I did not say anything about what had happened here last night, and I think, don't you agree, Max?" she glanced at my uncle, "that it would be as well not to mention the incident to anyone."

Max nodded.

"Yes, you are quite right, my dear. Sally is a nervous creature, and in her present condition, if she knew that there had been a break in so close to her own home, she might get very upset."

"I don't think Sally has anything to worry about," remarked Leo. "From what I have seen of the Villa Magnolia's defense system, no unwanted person could possibly break in!"

He turned to me. "Just wait until you see it, Melissa! You would think that royalty stayed there! Since the last spate of kidnappings on the island, because he knew how nervous Sally felt, especially when he is away so often on business trips, Devlin arranged for every safeguard he could think of! There are rolls of barbed wire along the tops of the garden walls, and guard dogs roam the grounds at night, to say nothing of an intricate alarm system in the house itself, which operates from a private dynamo, and which connects directly with the police station!"

He shook his head. "Yes," he continued, "I would imagine that the inmates of the Villa Magnolia are even better guarded than the Crown Jewels!"

EIGHT

Max reluctantly went indoors to tidy himself, followed by Jake and Leo, while Jane and I went to put away our morning's purchases in the pantry.

"It is a pity Richard Devlin is away at the moment," observed Jane as she showed me what items were kept in the various cupboards. "He and Max get on very well together, and Max doesn't like visiting his home when he is away. He is actually rather shy of the three women there."

"Max has never been a lady's man," I told her. "Sometimes I wonder if all my mother's attempts to get him married off when he was younger, has something to do with this!"

Jane laughed. "I've heard about that!" she said as we went upstairs to change. "I told him your mother was only doing it for his own good! He definitely needs someone to look after him!"

We parted company at the top of the stairs, and entering my bedroom I caught an unexpected glimpse of myself in the wardrobe mirror.

I grimaced. No matter how much I prettied myself, and no matter what I wore, I would never be able to transform myself into a glamour girl! I was not tall enough, I was too chubby cheeked, and I was too spontaneous in action ever to acquire the sophisticated poise which glamor requires.

Not that it mattered what I looked like this morning, I told myself. There was no one here who would spare me a second glance. Jake had his Jane, Leo was apparently under Bettina's spell, and apart from my uncle, the only other male I would meet would be young Dirk, and he was not likely to notice if his future tutor was plain or pretty!

I was not sure what to wear. My white, one-piece swimsuit with its matching, hip length beach jacket, would be ideal for lazing by the pool, but I could not sit at the luncheon table in a wet costume! From my small selection of clothes, I decided to wear the white cotton, full-skirted dress, with a low, boatline neck and broderie anglaise bodice, which I had bought in Montreux the previous week. It made me look more youthful than ever, I thought, as I brushed out my hair, but at least it showed up the delicate tan I had acquired that morning, and emphasised my small waist.

"I do like your dress!" Jane approved as I met her in the downstairs hall. "It makes you look so cool and petite!"

"You look very nice too, Jane!" Max told her, gallantly taking her arm and ushering her out of the door, before she could find fault with the outrageous scarlet tie with pink elephants on it, which he had raked out from heaven knew where!

Jake and I followed behind them as they walked down the dirt track which led to the entrance to the villa next door. After a couple of minutes we came to an archway in the high wall which surrounded the garden. A high, narrow-

76

barred gate blocked our way into the drive, but Max tugged at a heavy chain which hung down one side of the post, to announce our arrival.

A bell clanged out, and before it had stopped ringing a couple of snarling alsatians came bounding down the driveway and jumped up against the gate, scratching at the bars with their forepaws, and all the time yelping and baying in a way which made my blood run cold.

A swarthy complexioned man with the broad shoulders and burly build of a prize fighter came striding toward us.

"Neptune! Jupiter! To heel, boys. To heel!" he called to the dogs as he neared the gate.

The dogs continued to snarl, but in more muted tones, and reluctantly slunk back to obey the command. The man snapped a double chain lead to their broad leather collars and secured them to a post at the side of the drive, before unlocking the gate, grunting a "Buon giorno Professore" to Max, as he turned the key.

"I see what you mean about the place being well guarded," I whispered to Jake as we stepped into the garden. "I would hate to meet up with either of these beauties in the dark!"

Jake took my arm and gave it a reassuring squeeze, and Leo muttered, as we heard the gate clang shut behind us, "I hope old Pino doesn't unleash his pets until we are at a safe distance! I have come here for my lunch, not to be made a meal of!"

We walked up the drive to another high wall, with another iron gate, but this one was not locked and Max pushed it open and ushered Jane ahead of him, to lead the way into a beautifully laid out, formal garden, where the cooling splash of a fountain mingled with the steady droning of bees as they sucked honey from the exotic flowers which bloomed in the crescent-shaped flowerbeds.

I now had my first sight of the villa, a two-storied building, which was Moorish in design, with white painted walls, and arched doorways and windows.

Sally Devlin, wearing a loose-fitting caftan of palest green came out of the house to greet us.

"I am so glad you could all come this morning," she smiled, as she led us back through the house, across a marble-floored hall, whose tinted glass dome dimmed the sunlight, to french windows which opened out onto a flagged patio, which, like ours, was shaded by a trellis covered with vines and jasmine and interspersed with the vivid blue trumpets of morning glory.

From this patio a flight of shallow steps led down to the back garden and a heart-shaped swimming pool, which was protected from the sea breezes by a high wall, and an even higher hedge of evergreen magnolias.

Bettina, Eve and Dirk were swimming in the pool, but they did not at first notice our arrival.

"Max," Sally took my uncle's arm as they walked to the side of the pool, where inflated air beds, deck chairs and cushions were laid out, and a table set with a selection of drinks was shaded from the sun by a giant sun umbrella, "I am sorry that Richard is away on location at the moment. He had hoped to fly back from Spain today, but the star he is working with has proved rather temperamental, and things are not going as smoothly as he had hoped."

"I thought he was going to the States?" said Max.

"He had hoped to spend a day or two at home before flying there," sighed Sally. "Now he is going direct from Madrid, which means I shall not see him for another ten days!" she shook her head. "Sometimes I think that I saw more of him before we were married!"

Bettina and Eve came swimming across the pool to say "hello," and Eve climbed out of the water and crossed to the bar, asking us what we wanted to drink.

"I think I shall join Dirk in the pool first," said Jake, waving to the boy who had remained standing at the far side of the pond.

"I am afraid he is in one of his moods," bemoaned Sally. "I have been trying to ignore it, but it isn't easy!"

"I'll soon chivvy him out of it," said Eve smugly, as she handed around the drinks. "I am used to handling him!"

She plunged back into the water, and with a superb crawl soon reached the spot where Dirk was now sitting, dabbling his toes in the pond.

A frown creased Sally's smooth brow. It was plain to see that she was not pleased with Eve's offer, although she tried to hide her annoyance by saying,

"Melissa, if you would like to have a swim before lunch, the changing rooms are over there, behind the tamarisk hedge."

"I'll show her the way," Jane scrambled to her

79

feet. "It is so hot I am dying to get into the water!"

By the time we had changed, Leo and Jake had joined Bettina in the pool, while Max relaxed on the air bed beside Sally's chair.

Eve had climbed the rungs to the lower of the two diving boards, and was demonstrating diving technique to Dirk, who was standing on the board behind her.

Jane and I paused beside Sally to watch the lesson, and as I stood there I overheard Sally say to my uncle as she too looked toward the diving board.

"I don't understand where I have gone wrong with Dirk, Max. Before I married his father, he and I got on very well together."

"And you will get on very well with him again." Max reassured her. "Give him time to readjust, Sally. Remember that where once you were a friend of the family, you are now that creature that fairy tales warn children against—the awful step-mother!" he joked. "Yes, my dear, just give him time to find out that you are still his friend."

"I shouldn't worry about Dirk, Mrs. Devlin," I put in a word. "It is quite usual for children of his age to go through several annoying and provocative stages. I should know!" I smiled. "Apart from being one of a family of four, and having had to suffer a lot of teasing and tantrums, I taught children of Dirk's age for a year at a primary school, and he is acting just as they did!"

She frowned up at me, as if she didn't quite believe me.

80

"It is true, Mrs. Devlin," I assured her. "What is more, you would not take his moods quite so much to heart if he was your son and not a very new step-son!"

Our conversation was interrupted by a shout from Dirk, who had climbed up to the highest diving board.

"Hey! Everyone watch me! I am going to dive from here!" He moved right to the edge of the plank, and Sally struggled out of the deck chair and stood up, calling,

"Dirk! No! You mustn't! You will hurt yourself!"

She glared angrily across at Eve who was sitting on the lower board. "Stop him, Eve!" she insisted. "You shouldn't have encouraged him to go up there!"

The words were hardly out of her mouth when Dirk, ignoring her entreaty, got into position for the dive, and Sally's hand went to her mouth to stifle a cry of alarm as he plunged into the pool.

Unfortunately the dive was not a good one. Dirk struck the water at a flattish angle which must have hurt his abdomen. Water splattered out in all directions, and as Sally hurried to the edge of the pool to kneel down anxiously to await the outcome, the boy surfaced, his face contorted with a mixture of pain and discomfiture and anger at his failure.

He swam scowling to the edge of the basin, not toward Sally, but to where Bettina and Leo were standing.

"Hard luck, son," commiserated Leo, but Bettina, believing herself to be the chosen comforter shot a smug smile at Sally, who was hurrying toward them, and put an arm round Dirk's shoulder saying,

"Poor Dirk, you made a real crash dive there!"

Dirk shoved her arm roughly to the side, and with a tearful sniff he pushed between her and Leo, and ran along the side of the pool, rudely shoving Sally out of his way as she in her turn tried to put a comforting arm around him.

Sally's face went white, and she half turned to follow him into the shrubbery where he had disappeared from view, but Max put a detaining hand on her arm.

"Leave him be," he advised. "He is a young man whose pride has been hurt more than his body, and at his age," he shook his head, "hurt pride can be a very painful experience!"

"Yes," agreed Jake, "Dirk needs a few minutes to cool down, in fact," he tactfully changed the subject, "we all need to cool down!

"Come on, Melissa!" he challenged me. "I'll race you across the pool!"

But although I plunged into the water after him, my heart was not in the race. I was thinking with pity of a small boy who was caught in a web of conflicting loves, for, in that moment there, by the pool side, after Dirk's disastrous plunge, I had become acutely aware that under their veneer of sweet friendship for each other, between Eve and Bettina and Sally, there was a feeling of intense jealously, a jealousy which centered around their own love for Dirk.

NINE

Fortunately Dirk quickly recovered from his tantrum and returned to join us in the pond for the quarter of an hour we spent there before going to the changing rooms to get dressed for the luncheon party.

The meal was served in the long, cool dining room which looked out over an inner courtyard where miniature orange trees grew in round green tubs. It was a leisurely affair, and the conversation, about holidays, and different national dishes, and the dress collections which Sally and Bettina had recently seen in Florence, would have gone down very well as a lesson in my class on etiquette at the Château.

Dirk, seated between his mother, who was at the head of the table, and Jake, paid more attention to his food than to the table talk, and the last hour of our visit to the Villa Magnolia sped past quickly and pleasantly.

When we were leaving, Leo asked Bettina if she would like to drive out with Jake and me to visit one of the nuraghe on the site where they were working, but she refused, saying she had a previous engagement.

"Could I come with you?" Dirk pushed forward eagerly. "I have never been inside a nuraghe."

"Now, Dirk," Sally chided him. "You can't invite yourself on someone else's outing!"

"In any case," put in Eve, "I thought you were going to come to Alghero with me and have one of your favorite ice creams at the Ciào Ciào."

Sally looked at Eve with annoyance. "I thought that you and I had arranged to go through the mail which piled up in our absence in Florence, this afternoon," she said sharply.

"I am sorry, Mrs. Devlin!" Eve was most contrite. "I forgot to mention to you that I had a telephone call from the manager of the Hotel Castello, asking me to go along there this afternoon, to check over the arrangements for the party Mr. Devlin is giving there on the 8th."

"Surely there is no need to go this afternoon!" Sally exclaimed. "The party isn't for another fortnight!"

"You can't make arrangements for such an important occasion overnight," said Eve knowledgeably. "They take a lot of planning, and I know that Richard—Mr. Devlin," she amended hastily, "likes these occasions to go without a hitch."

"Oh, very well!" Sally acquiesced. "We can attend to the mail when you return."

"Run and get ready, Dirk," Eve turned to the little boy. "We shall be leaving in a few minutes."

Dirk was still gazing hopefully at Jake, who looked across at me, his eyebrows raised, and getting the message, I said quickly.

"I would be very pleased if Dirk could come with us," I said to his step-mother. "An outing like this would give us an opportunity of getting to know one another, and we might even do some nature study!" I ruffled Dirk's still damp hair.

Sally's face lit up.

"Are you sure you wouldn't mind taking him? I know it is the kind of outing which appeals to him."

"Of course we don't mind!" I shook my head. "And we promise to see he doesn't get into mischief!"

"We shall be back here by six o'clock," added Jake. "Is that all right?"

Sally nodded.

Dirk was hopping from one foot to the other with delight, but Eve looked rather taken aback at the turn of events, although surely she must have realized that to a small boy, a day in the country, exploring old ruins and chasing butterflies and moths was a much more exciting prospect than sedately eating ice-cream at a local café!

Sally walked down the drive with us, and stood in the roadway until we had reached our own gateway so that she could wave goodbye to Dirk.

I was surprised when I learned that Max and Jane were not coming with us, but they had arranged to go to Sassari to visit a friend of Max's who was a professor at the university there, and another keen archaeologist, and they set off before we were ready to leave, because Jake advised me to change from my light cotton dress and high-heeled sandals into clothes and shoes which would be more suitable for the cross country walk we would have to make, and for scrambling around old ruins.

I was looking forward to the afternoon's excursion, for my uncle had told me quite a lot about the amazing Sardinian nuraghe, which are to be found all over the island, and whose strange, cylindrical shapes remind me of the bee-hive shaped Scottish brochs.

Now that Dirk was coming with us, Jake decided not to go to see the ruined towers on the site where Max was working, but to visit one that was nearer to Alghero, in case we didn't get back to the Villa Magnolia by six, as we had promised Sally.

We drove along the coast road, through Alghero, and out toward the airport, and while Dirk prattled happily to Leo, I looked about me with interest as Jake told me the names of the places we were passing.

After a time we came to a road which was bordered with flowering oleanders. There were such masses of blossom, in colors ranging from white through pink to deepest crimson, that I exclaimed in delight, and Jake smiled at me, a warm, affectionate smile that stirred my blood, and said.

"So you are still the same flower daft little Melissa!" he shook his head. "I would stop the car and pick you a garland, my love, but the flowers would be dead before we got back to the house, and in any case," he added, "the oleander is a poisonous plant to both man and beast, didn't you know?"

I shook my head. "Isn't it sad that some of the loveliest plants are the deadliest ones?"

"A form of self-protection, perhaps, the way roses have thorns!" he replied.

We drove on down the floral avenue, and passed a group of tumble-down cottages, outside of which a small urchin was standing, waving to us to stop.

When we did so, he indicated a pile of large, green watermelons by the side of the road.

"Only 250 lire!" he told us. "Very ripe, very juicy, very good!" he poked his head into the car, and Dirk gaped with curiosity at the cheerful, bare-footed youngster, whose worn and faded T-shirt stretched too tightly over his narrow chest as he waved his thin brown arms to us, saying in pleading tones. "Please signore, signorina, only 250 lire!"

"If I can't have my bouquet," I touched Jake's arm lightly with my fingers, "how about a watermelon instead?"

Jake laughed. "Very well!"

I got out of the car and crossed to the pile of fruit, where Jake joined me, to help me select one which was ready to eat. In the end, because the lad could not change the note we gave him, we decided to take two melons, one to eat when we reached the nuraghe, the other to take home for lunch the following day.

Dirk was delighted with the episode. He had never bought fruit at the roadside before, never even been to the local market to buy it there, and hadn't even visited the weekly market in Alghero where, according to Jake, you could buy all sorts of interesting things, like cork and coral and pottery and home-made cheeses, all of which could be bartered for.

I promised him I would take him to both mar-

kets, to broaden his education, as I put it. I
thought it would be good for him once in a while
to escape from the glass house conditions he
seemed to have lived in all his life, to see how
those who were less well off than he was, conducted their lives.

We drove on for another mile or so, until we
came to a broken down gateway, leading into a
field, and here we stopped and parked the car.

"There it is, Melissa!" he pointed across the
field. "Your first nuraghe!"

We walked across the rough and stony ground
toward the prehistoric ruin. In spite of the arid
conditions, the field was carpeted with an amazing variety of wild flowers. There were trails of
tri-colored convolvulus, tall yellow thistles, and
clusters of sky blue chicory, and not far from the
nuraghe, upright as a sentinel on guard was a tall
flowering agave, whose spiky leaved base was
thick with dust from the sandy area in front of the
ruin.

As usual, I had forgotten to bring my camera,
and when I bemoaned the fact, Jake laughed and
said that no harm had been done

"You can come back here another day and take
photographs, Melissa. This building has stood for
thousands of years, so it is unlikely to collapse
overnight!" he teased, taking me by the arm.
"Come on in and have a look around the inside of
it," he urged me forward, adding, "Leo you can
keep an eye on young Dirk!"

Jake had to duck his head as we entered the
tiny opening which led into the building. Coming
from the bright sunlight into the deep shadows in-

side, it took my eyes a few seconds to be able to make out that we were standing in a kind of circular hall, strewn with stones which, through the ages, had fallen from the dome shaped roof, most of which now lay open to the sky.

Jake led me through a narrow corridor to a staircase within the thickness of the outer wall, which led up to the higher chambers of the building. The steps, formed from huge, irregular stones, were very steep, and I understood now why Jake had insisted I put on my denims again, for there were times when I had to scramble upwards on my hands and knees.

However the effort was worth while, for the view from the top was superb, and even Dirk, whose legs were shorter than mine, and who must have had quite a struggle to get up, was delighted with his achievement.

Looking at his dusty face, his sand-stained shirt, and the grazes on the fine skin of his knees from his contact with the rough hewn stones, I wondered what his step-mother or Eve would have said if they could have seen him at this moment, but why should I worry about them? The boy was enjoying himself as a boy should, and that was important.

"Are the other nuraghe much like this one?" I asked.

Jake nodded. "More or less. They date from about 1000 BC, and we have assumed that they were the defensive towers for villages of stone huts built near them. The people who lived in these communities were mainly agriculturists, but they must have had a certain amount of wealth too, to feel the need to protect themselves with these towers.

"The part of their history in which Max is interested is the later stage, and on the site where we are at present working, we have found more of those curious votive figurines, of warriors and deities and priests, which show a strong Etruscan influence."

"Ah, now I understand why he came here!" I nodded. "The riddle of the Etruscans has always fascinated him, as it fascinates so many people."

Leo and Dirk started the descent, but Jake and I lingered for a few more minutes, to look out across the fields to the broad expanse of sea beyond the high cliffs, where a couple of sleek, gray warships were moving in the direction of the harbor at Alghero.

"The night clubs will be busy tonight, if the men from these ships get shore leave!" observed Jake.

"Are there night clubs in Alghero?" I asked, surprised.

"Alghero has a very gay night life!" he assured me. "Later in the week, once the fleet has departed, I shall take you on a tour of them!"

Through an opening in the wall, we could see that Leo and Dirk had now reached the foot of the stairs, and they stepped out into the field, where Dirk, with a shout of delight, was now pursuing a fluttering white butterfly.

"He is enjoying himself, isn't he?" Jake smiled at me. "I am glad you asked him to come with us."

"It seemed a shame that he was going to have to spend an afternoon like this, eating ice-cream with

Eve!" I shook my head. "I imagined how you, or any of my brothers would have felt at Dirk's age, faced with such a prospect, so I took pity on him!"

Jake glanced at his watch. "I think it is time we got back to the car and opened up our watermelon," he decided. "This climb has made me quite thirsty, and there is no thirst quencher to beat a nice, juicy watermelon!"

Going down the rough steps was even more difficult than scrambling up them. I thought we would never get to the foot, but at last there was only one more large awkward step to descend.

I was so pleased to be almost back on ground level, that instead of stepping carefully as I had done till now, I decided to jump down. I misjudged the height of the stone, and landed with a painful thud on my heels on top of a stone which had been worn to a slippery smoothness.

My feet shot from under me, and I would have had a nasty fall, if Jake hadn't heard my gasp of pain as I landed, and turned round to grab at me before I lost my balance.

"Melissa! You little idiot!" he held me tight, looking down at me and shaking his head. "Why do you always have to be in such a hurry to get places!"

I looked up at him, very conscious of the strength of his arms around me, very conscious of his closeness as he continued to hold me tight, very conscious of the peculiar gleam in his eyes as he stared down at me, very conscious that I wanted, more than anything, to go on standing like this, with Jake's arms around me, with my head tilted, as I was tilting it now, in expectation of a kiss, but as Jake bent his head down, so that his face was almost touching mine, I remembered Jane, Leo's sister, who was secretly engaged to Jake, who loved him, who would have hated to see me now, provoking her lover to kiss me.

With a murmur of protest, I pushed myself free, saying, crossly, hoping to make him think that he had misinterpreted my moment of weakness.

"For goodness' sake, Jake! I am a big girl now, and quite able to pick myself up after a fall without your help!"

Without another glance at him, I went stumbling out of the shadowy tower into the brilliance of the Sardinian sunlight.

TEN

"Look what I have found! Look what I have found!" Dirk shouted as he came racing up to me. "Do you think it is a Roman coin? Do you think it is valuable?"

He shoved a round, dirt encrusted piece of metal into my hand and looked up at me eagerly.

I held the disc in the palm of my hand, and stared down at it blankly. I was still thinking distractedly of those last seconds in the nuraghe when I had come so close to betraying my feelings to Jake. Thank goodness it had been dark and shadowy in the ruin, so that Jake could not have read the message in my eyes, could only have heard the forced annoyance in my voice as I pulled away from him. My cheeks still felt hot with shame as I remembered how I had tilted my face toward his.

"Well?" demanded Dirk impatiently. "Is it a Roman coin? Is it worth lots and lots of money?"

Behind us I could hear the clatter of stones as Jake came stepping out of the old tower, and pulling myself together with an effort, I said, in a tone that surprised me by its normality.

"I am afraid I am not an authority on Roman coins, Dirk. You had better ask Jake or Leo about it. That is their line!"

"Not quite," said Leo, coming over to join us. "We are only amateurs at this sort of thing. Uncle Max is the expert. You take it home and show it to him."

"Can we look for more?" Dirk demanded eagerly.

Jake shook his head. "Some other time. Melissa was on her way to divide up the watermelon when you stopped her, because it will soon be time for us to return home."

"I think that Melissa should do a repair job on her trouser leg before we go," grinned Leo, "or she might be mistaken for another melon seller!"

I looked down at my knees and gasped with annoyance. One trouser leg had been ripped above the knee, exposing a bruised area of flesh where I had bumped against the jagged step as I fell forward. Moreover, my trousers and blouse were dusty and dirtied from scrambling up and down the steps in the nuraghe, and as Leo had unkindly indicated, I did look rather like one of the peasant urchins!

"I hope you haven't cut your leg," said Jake solicitously. "Let me have a look. It wouldn't do to get dirt into an open wound."

I sat down on a boulder and rolled up the torn trouser leg to examine my knee, but fortunately the skin hadn't been broken, although the area of bruising was quite extensive.

I rolled up the other trouser leg, so that both were level in length, brushed my knees clean with a paper tissue, and dusted the loose grit and sand from my blouse.

"Does that look better?" I cocked my head at Leo, but it was Jake who said with a smile.

"Now you look like Tom Sawyer!"

I smiled at his remark, but as our glances met, Jake frowned suddenly, and such an odd gleam came into his eyes, that I was grateful to Dirk for pushing his way between us, grabbing at my hand and saying impatiently, "Do hurry! I want my piece of watermelon! I am dying of thirst!"

We divided up the melon, and when we had finished eating, Dirk planted the seeds from his portion in the ground near where the car was parked, before we set off on our return journey.

I chose to sit with Dirk in the back seat for the homeward trip, and I was glad of his ceaseless talk. If the afternoon had been a near disastrous one for me, in more ways than one, for Dirk it had been a complete success, and when we stopped at the entrance to the Villa Magnolia, and waited for the guard to come and open the gate, he eagerly asked Jake and Leo if they would take him with them to the place where they were looking for buried treasures, as he called it.

"We shall have to ask Professor Little about that," Jake told him. "He is the man in charge. But if you like," he added kindly, "and if your mother gives her permission, you can join us at our barbecue on Wednesday, how about that?"

"Great!" he exclaimed. "You can ask Sally-mum now if it will be all right," he glanced through the bars of the gate. "Here she comes now!"

Sally was quite agreeable, especially when she learned that there would be some of Carlo's young relatives at the picnic, although she said to Dirk.

95

"I do hope you didn't pester Mr. Carnegie and Miss Gilchrist to take you on another outing!"

Jake grinned. "Dirk wants to come and work with us, and find more buried treasure! I don't think he realizes what dull work it can be at times!"

"But I am good at finding things!" he said, "Look, Sally-mum, look what I found today!" he held out the old coin for her inspection.

"I hope you have thanked your friends for giving you such a pleasant afternoon," she said to him.

"Yes, he has," I told her. "And we enjoyed having him with us."

"For that matter," Jake smiled at her, "I think it would be a good idea if you and Bettina could come along on Wednesday as well—Eve too, of course, if she is free," he added as an afterthought. "It is actually going to be an evening picnic—a barbecue—on the beach near Boza."

Sally hesitated.

"It sounds like fun, Jake," she said. "But I am not quite sure what my plans are for Wednesday. I shall have to check with Eve. She keeps me right about these things," she smiled. "In fact, Eve arranges most of my social life for me, much as she was used to doing for Richard." She giggled. "I still can't get used to having a social secretary run my life, but I expect I shall have to!" She slipped an arm round Dirk's shoulder. "I shall phone you this evening and let you know what is what."

"There is no hurry," said Jake. "No doubt we shall be seeing you before Wednesday in any case."

We got back into the car, and Sally and Dirk waved goodbye as we drove back up the road.

"I do hope the girls can come on Wednesday," said Leo as we turned into the driveway of the Villa Gelsomino.

"What you mean, Leo, is that you hope Bettina will join us!" said Jake drily. "But I wouldn't get too involved with her, if I was you," he advised. "She isn't your type."

"Any pretty girl is my type," Leo joked and winked at me. "Isn't that so, Melissa?"

"Any pretty girl is any man's type!" I replied. "You men are all Don Juans at heart!"

"What? Are there no Prince Charmings?" teased Jake as he stopped the car outside the villa.

"If there are, I have still to find mine!" I said lightly, as I opened the door. "They seem to be very few and far between!"

"Max and Jane haven't got back yet," observed Leo, glancing at the empty garage. "Do you think they will be gone long?"

"I expect they will stay for dinner with Bruno. You know what Max and he are like when they get together. They never stop talking, and they lose track of time, and Jane is every bit as bad!" Jake smiled and shook his head. "If they have got around to their usual arguments as to who were the Etruscans and where did they come from, it will be the small hours before we see them!"

I looked at the two men.

"In that case, if you give me time to change from my peasant rags," I grimaced childishly at Jake, "I shall prepare our dinner. What time do you want to eat?"

"No, no!" said Jake firmly. "We can't have that, can we, Leo? After all, Melissa, your stint as chief cook does not officially start until Monday, so we shall take you out for a meal tonight!"

"It seems silly to go out for dinner when I think of all the lovely food Jane and I bought today," I demurred. "I don't mind preparing something for this evening."

Leo chuckled. "Don't let Jake fool you into thinking we were going to do you a favor, Melissa! Saturday nights we always eat out at the Mermaid's Cave. It has become part of the routine!"

"Most of the English speaking colony in Alghero meet at the Mermaid on a Saturday," Jake confirmed.

"It has a friendly atmosphere, the food is good, and there is dancing," added Leo. "It is a pity we shall miss the star turn tonight!" he grinned. "Jane and Jake usually have the floor to themselves for the tango. They dance together like professionals!"

I managed to keep on smiling, but in reality I wanted to cry out in protest. The tango was a dance Jake and I had practiced together in the past, a dance for which we had created a special new routine, our dance, I had unwittingly thought of it through the years. Our special party piece.

"If we are going dancing, I had better go up and change," I said in a brittle voice. "I am stiff all over from my fall in that decrepit old ruin, and I shall need a long soak in the bath to ease my aches and pains!"

"Don't be too long," said Jake, "and don't leave

the bathroom snowed under with talcum as Jane does. I think she puts it on the floor to dry it as well as herself!"

Jane, I thought. Always Jane. She seemed to be at the forefront of his mind all the time!

I trailed drearily up the stairs, to undress and run the water into the bath. My spirits were at such a low ebb I had no desire to go out dancing this evening. All I wanted to do was lie on and on in the soft, blissful comfort of the foaming bath.

Leo rattled at the bathroom door.

"Hurry up there, Melissa. Jake has made up some sandwiches and the coffee will be ready any minute. We thought it would be a good idea to have a bite to eat now, since dinner at the Mermaid is not served until fairly late."

Reluctantly I got out of the warm, scented water, quickly patted my body dry with the fluffy bath sheet, and wrapping my terry cloth robe around me, went to my room to dress.

Leo, who was standing at the foot of the stairs now, called up to me when he heard me leave the bathroom. "If you are decent, come down as you are, Melissa. You can titivate yourself later. We are eating in the kitchen to save time and labor!"

I glanced at myself briefly in the dressing table mirror. I did not look very chic in my shapeless bathrobe, my head enclosed in a lacy, plastic shower cap, but what did it matter? Jake and Leo were used to seeing me in my less glamorous moments, and at least I was what Leo would term "decent!"

Jake's idea of sandwiches was a hunk of the local crusty bread, covered with a wedge of the local goat cheese and piled with chutney. They could not be eaten gracefully, but they did taste good, and since we were all hungry after our day in the open, we ate them greedily.

"I think that you will have to have another bath, Melissa!" Jake chaffed me as I wiped traces of the brown chutney from my nose and chin.

"Look who is talking!" I jibed. "At least I didn't get any of the stuff in my hair! Shall I run the water into the bath for you, when I go up to wash my face, or do you think you look elegant enough to go to the Mermaid's Cave as you are?"

"That reminds me!" Leo interrupted our joking. "The Mermaid is not a place that goes in for formal evening wear, in case you were thinking along those lines, Melissa," he told me.

"That white dress you wore this morning would do," said Jake, and I gave him a surprised look, for he had seemed to pay so little attention to me at the Devlins that I had thought he had not noticed what I was wearing.

ELEVEN

The Mermaid's Cave was situated in the basement of one of the old buildings which overlooked the sea front, a few hundred yards away from the Piazza Sulis. It was one of the new night spots in Alghero, and catered mainly to the less sophisticated tourist, and the locals

The steps leading down to it were steep and dimly lit, and I had to cling to the iron hand rail, ignoring the offer of Jake's helping hand, to make sure that I did not repeat my undignified fall of the afternoon.

Inside the long, low ceilinged cellar, the lighting was equally dim, except for the bar at the far corner, and it was not until a waiter had guided me to a table at the edge of the minute dancing area, and I had sat down for a few seconds that my eyes became accustomed to the dimness and I was able to look around me and study the decor.

The walls of the "Cave" were of rough-hewn stones, and draped with fishing nets in which lobsters, and giant crabs and revolting plastic octopuses were enmeshed. Small alcoves in the wall had been glassed over, and in the water-filled area behind the glass, concealed lighting revealed all manner of exotic fish darting in and out of wavy seaweeds and miniature banks of coral.

Behind the bar, the wall was smoothly plastered, and painted over with mermaids whose like I am sure Hans Andersen never dreamed of, for they were more like bacchantes with fish tails than the gentle, innocent mermaid statue which mourns over the harbor at Copenhagen.

To the right of the bar, a four piece band of men dressed in what I took to be the local costume, idly tuned up their instruments as they talked to the barman, and from the kitchen quarters, behind a heavy drape which covered an aperture not far from where we were sitting, came the clatter of plates and pans and the appetizing smell of cooking.

The night club was packed to capacity, except for an empty table next to ours, on which there was a reserved notice, and the hubbub of voices and laughter was deafening.

A waiter came up to take our order. Jake said that we were waiting for the arrival of some friends, but meanwhile, we would take an apéritif.

"What would you like, Melissa? A glass of the local wine, or a cocktail? Tony mixes a splendid Alexander," he suggested.

"I'll have a Campari, please!"

"And a couple of beers for us," Jake told the man.

"And a bottle of the usual for us, Tony!" said a voice, and I looked up into Carlo Roncardi's smiling eyes as he touched me on the shoulder, and said.

"Do you mind if we join you?"

He signaled to another waiter to push our table next to the vacant one alongside, adding, "There will be plenty of room for the Professor and Jane when they arrive."

"They are not joining us tonight," said Jake, standing up to greet the two women who had come with Carlo and his friend. "They went to visit Bruno in Sassari."

"But Bettina is coming along later, or so she said," Leo indicated the vacant chair by his side.

Carlo introduced me to his brother Gianni, and Gianni's wife, Giulia, and Giulia's young and pretty sister Angelina, but the band, which had started to play a noisy cha cha, made polite exchanges quite impossible, so we all sat silently smiling at one another, until Carlo asked if I would care to dance with him.

"With your permission," he added courteously to Jake, who shrugged and said with a smile.

"With or without my permission Melissa would have accepted your invitation! She loves to dance."

"In any case, Jake is not my keeper!" I said lightly. "So you need not consult him in future when you want to ask me to dance!"

"So?" Carlo's eyes gleamed as we stepped on to the dance floor, and responded to the rhythm of the music, "Jake is not special to you? He has always talked about you so much, I suspected that you and he had some sort of understanding, no?"

"No!" I said firmly. "We are just, as we say back home, good friends!"

"Good!" Carlo twinkled down at me. "Then he will not mind when he is busy with his work, if I take you to show you the beauty spots on the island that we talked about last night?"

I hesitated.

"I should like that very much," I said slowly, "but I am not here on holiday and my time is not my own, didn't you know? Apart from helping with the cooking, in a few days I shall be working in the mornings, as tutor to Dirk Devlin."

"Yes. I know about that, as I know about most things which take place in his area," he said frankly. "It is my business."

"Your business?" I queried. "What business is that? You are not the local gossip columnist by any chance, are you?" I laughed.

"Not quite," he smiled, but at the same time, he did not enlighten me as to what his occupation was, merely saying, "people interest me. That is why I studied psychology at the university here and in Scotland."

"Why Scotland?"

"I have cousins there, in Edinburgh. It was an excuse to pay them a long visit?" he said lightly.

"You seem to have cousins and sisters and brothers all over the place!" I remarked. "Jake told me that the estate agent who arranged about the villa is your cousin. The police captain is your brother-in-law. Your sister is married to the architect who designed the Villa Magnolia and two of the hotels we passed on our way to the Palma Nova nuraghe this afternoon."

"So that is where you went!" he side-tracked me. "What did you think of the old tower? It was interesting, yes?"

I nodded breathlessly. I had not danced for some time, and I was out of training for this cha cha which seemed to go on and on.

"I should like to see one in a better state of preservation, if that is possible," I gasped.

He nodded. "I shall take you to one of the ones near Nuoro."

At that moment the music stopped, Carlo smiled down at me, and slipping his hand round my waist, led me back to our table where Bettina, who had newly arrived, was being introduced by Jake to Carlo's relatives.

"Isn't Eve coming along tonight?" Carlo slipped into a chair between Bettina and myself.

Bettina laughed.

"Eve is in the doghouse!" She seemed to enjoy this fact, judging from her tone. "She has to work tonight to get Richard's mail up to date!"

"Surely she is entitled to time off!" I said indignantly.

Bettina glanced at me and said with a shrug. "Eve is not exactly overworked, Melissa. On the contrary, especially when Richard is away she has a lot of time off, but from time to time, Sally likes to show her who is boss, especially when Eve tries to take advantage of her, as she did this afternoon."

"I thought she was going to see about arrangements for a party or something, at the Castello?" said Leo.

"She may have spent a few minutes there," Bettina said, "but when she came back to the house, it was very obvious where she had spent most of the afternoon. At Francesco's!"

"Who is Francesco?" I asked curiously.

"The hair stylist," said Bettina impatiently. "You must have heard about him! He is THE person to go to at the moment. The joke was," she reverted to her story, "Eve could not deny that she had been to him, because he had created a fabulous new style for her—quite taken away the secretary image to make her look rather Voguish, if you know what I mean, and I think Sally was a bit jealous. I know I was," she said frankly.

"Ah! Francesco!" breathed Giulia. "How I wish I could afford to have him style my hair!"

Leo looked at Bettina. "If he is such a wonderful man, what is he doing, working in a place like Alghero—I don't mean to be denigrating to your home town, Carlo," he added quickly. "But you know what I mean."

"His main establishment is in Rome," explained Bettina, "but in the summer months he works in the branch at Porto Cervo, on the Costa Smeralda, where most of his rich and famous customers spend their summer vacation. Once a week, for the benefit of a few very special customers like the Estes and the Balfours, and of course, because of Richard, Sally, who have villas near Alghero, he sets up shop, so to speak, in the Hotel Marengo. As Richard's sister-in-law, I managed to get onto his list, and Eve did too, so every Friday," she smiled, "like three little lambs for the shearing, we go along to the Marengo for him to perform his wonders on us!"

The music started up again, making further conversation difficult, so I turned my attention to the menu which lay on the table in front of me. The names of many of the dishes meant nothing to me, and Carlo asked if he could order for me,

106

bending close to my ear to explain what the dishes consisted of.

Leo and Bettina, and Jake and Angelina got up to dance, followed to the floor by Carlo's brother and his wife.

By this time the place was so packed it seemed impossible that anyone else could be squeezed in. Business at the bar was brisk, and I noticed among its customers a number of white uniformed sailors, whom I took to be on shore leave from the warships which we had noticed anchoring off Alghero that afternoon.

Because of the crowds and because of the stuffiness, the manager flung open two doors on either side of the rostrum where the band was playing. These doors led out onto a small courtyard, where more tables were set up, and candles were put in saucers in the center of them, to give some light.

The waiter brought our order, and between courses we danced or talked, and I asked Bettina if Sally ever joined the crowd at the Mermaid on a Saturday.

"If Richard is at home, she does, but when he is away, she is very circumspect. You have to be in her position," Bettina added. "The eye of the gossip columnist is always upon you, and if Sally happened to glance twice at another man, however casually, she would be accused of having an affair with him. I know!" she spoke with some bitterness. "The number of times, after my sister's death, that it was reported that Richard and I were going to get married, couldn't be counted."

She stirred the last of the ice-cream in her dish, until it turned into a liquid mass as she added.

"Before I was the target, they had Richard secretly married to Eve!" she shook her head. "It was because of these rumors that he asked me to join his household, plus the fact he felt it would be nice for Dirk to have me around. Poor soul! He didn't realize he was only going to cause more scandal, but he said if I could take it, he could, because he knew I had had difficulty trying to get a job after my husband's death, and he felt that by providing a home for me, he was helping me out.

"He is rather a pet, you know. He could no more ask me to go than he could have dismissed Eve when the rumors started to fly! But was I glad," she said with a smile, "when he met and married Sally! That put an end to all the silly speculations of the gossip columns, even although there are times when I think Sally wonders how much truth there was in the stories, and would dearly love to show Eve at least, the door!"

"What is this talk about gossip columnists?" Carlo turned his attention to us. "Melissa seems fascinated by them," he smiled at me. "She even thought I was one of them!"

Jake laughed.

"That is not quite Carlo's line!" he held out a hand to pull me to my feet. "Come on, my love, it is time we had a dance together. You have been evading that pleasure all evening."

The band struck up a conga, and led by one of the managers of the club the dance began, with the guests leaving their tables as he jogged past them, to add to the growing tail of laughing, swaying dancers.

The leader led the way in and out of the tables,

around the bar, out of one of the doors leading to the courtyard, and in the other. As more and more people joined in the fun I found myself separated from Jake, who was in front of me, and Carlo, whose hands had been lightly clasping my waist from behind.

I looked around to see where they had got to as the line wove its way hither and thither, changing direction abruptly from time to time, so that we never quite knew where we were going to go.

The music grew louder and louder, faster and faster, the dancers merrier, and the serpent became a hydra-headed monster with break away groups dancing off in different directions. I found myself in one of the break away groups which was led by a sailor, and another sailor who was jogging behind me, his hands on my waist, urged me out into the candle-lit patio, and away from the brightness of the light from the bar, which flooded out through the open door, round and round the tables so quickly that we soon shed the other few dancers who had tagged on to us; in and out between the pillars supporting a trellis roof, and past the trellised way to a gate in the back wall. The leading sailor pranced through the gate, into a shadowy lane, and I let go of him, and turned to retreat to the patio, but the sailor dancing behind me had other ideas.

His grasp around my waist tightened, and he pushed me forward out into the unlit alley with a force that sent me reeling forward.

"For goodness' sake!" I rounded on him angrily, but anger gave way to fear when I heard him clang the door shut, and realized that I was quite alone in this lonely lane, except for the two sailors who had deliberately led me here!

From over the wall, the gay music of the conga came in waves of sound, mingling with the cheerful shouts and laughter of the dancers who were enjoying themselves in the courtyard.

I stood, my back pressed against the wall, staring with terrified eyes at the taller of the two men, the one who had closed the gate, who was walking slowly towards me. There was not enough light in the lane to make out his features. All I could see was the white of his teeth as his mouth opened in a snarling smile, when he whipped a white scarf from the bodice of his tunic, and holding the strip of cloth in both hands, he approached me, as the intruder in my room the previous evening had approached me. At the same time, the smaller sailor made a grab at my arm. I had a vague glimpse of shaggy blond hair and a shaggy blond beard as I tried to wrench myself from his grasp, but he twisted my arm behind my back, to urge me toward the other man, and unable to free myself, I opened my mouth and screamed at the top of my voice, for someone to come to my aid.

I screamed again, but tonight there was no one to hear my scream, for who would listen to one more cry among the cries and shouts and laughter rising in the air from the revelers in the courtyard of the Mermaid's Cave?

No, tonight I could not expect anyone to come to my aid, and yet I screamed again, as much in outrage as in fear, and with an angry movement which took both men by surprise, I lowered my head as I pulled free from the blond sailor, and catapulted forward below the level of the threatening scarf to strike the man who was holding it in the abdomen, with all the strength of my hard young head!

He gasped and doubled up with pain, and I darted past him, toward the mouth of the alley, expecting at any moment to be caught and held by his companion as I struggled along the cobbled way on my high-heeled sandals, all the time shouting for help at the top of my voice in a mixture of Italian and English, yet knowing, with growing despair, that no one could hear me, except the man who was coming pounding down the alley in my pursuit.

TWELVE

The man was now so close I could hear his panting breath, and when he shot out a hand and grabbed at my arm, I was too exhausted with emotion even to scream. I felt faint, and as weakness radiated through all my limbs, my knees threatened to give way under me, and it was impossible to drag myself forward another step.

"Melissa!" A man's voice cried out at me, but at first I was too overcome to recognize it.

"Melissa!" my name was repeated, and my captor pulled me round to face him, and hold me close against his chest in a pair of strong, comforting arms.

At first I couldn't believe that it was Jake who was holding me, Jake who was repeating my name. When I did, I was so overcome with relief, that I burst into tears, and clung to him, fiercely, as a shipwrecked sailor clings to the spar in the ocean which could save him.

"Melissa, it is all right," he comforted me, holding my head against his shoulder, stroking my hair with his fingers. "You are quite safe now!"

I could not speak for a moment, and even after my sobbing stopped, and strength returned to my trembling limbs, I made no effort to talk or push myself away from his embrace. I felt so secure, so safe, so at home in the circle of his arms, that I wanted to go on and on, savoring the pleasure of the experience.

It was when I heard the sound of other approaching footsteps that I finally reluctantly pushed Jake from me, and looked up at him, to say with an attempt at a joke, remembering an old childhood game we had often played together, with my brothers.

"The cowboys arrived in time once more, didn't they?"

Jake was not in a joking mood.

"What on earth possessed you, Melissa, to go off on your own with that bunch of drunken sailors?" he asked harshly.

"Jake!" I protested. "I didn't realize I was on my own with them! I thought at first you and some of the other dancers were tagging on behind! It was too dark in the patio to see what was happening."

A man came to a halt behind Jake, and for a frightened moment, as I glanced over his shoulder. I thought that it was the taller of the two sailors, but as Jake turned to him, from the swaying light of the lamp at the mouth of the alley, I recognized Carlo, and coming up behind him was his brother.

"They got away!" announced Carlo, tight-lipped. "This alley is like a rabbit warren, with paths and courtyards, but we have alerted the police, and they will search the area."

Carlo stepped close to me and looked down at me, asking.

"Did you get a good look at them, Melissa?

114

Would you be able to identify them if you saw them again?"

I bit my lip thoughtfully. "I don't think so. No, Carlo," I shook my head. "I doubt it. I wasn't paying much attention to them when they pushed their way into the conga line, one in front of me, the other behind me. They were just men in white naval uniforms—"

"But when they brought you out here, into the alley?" his eyes held mine. "They must have been close enough to you then, must have been eyeing you—"

I shivered again, remembering the scene, and Jake caught my hand, and held it warmly.

"Don't you think we should go back to The Mermaid, Carlo? You can ask your questions there," he went on. "Melissa is chilled with shock, and needs time, and something hot to drink, to help her recover from her unpleasant experience."

"No!" I protested. "I can't go back to The Mermaid looking like this!" I pulled myself away from Jake to indicate where the shoulder of my dress had been ripped away in my struggle to free myself from my assailants.

"My God!" exclaimed Jake hoarsely. "Do you mean to say that they, that they—" he choked over his final words.

"Yes," I said shakily. "They tried to kill me. One of them held me, while the other one came up to me, holding a long scarf between his hands, just like the intruder last night!"

I stared wide-eyed, shivering, from Jake to Carlo, while Gianni let out a low gasp of anger.

"That's enough, Melissa!" said Jake roughly. "Try to forget about it for the moment."

He looked at Carlo. "Let's get her back to the villa. Jane may be home by now, and able to take care of her."

Carlo nodded. "Si. We shall do that. My car is only a few yards away, around the corner. Gianni," he turned to his brother. "Tell the others what has happened. Find out if any of them noticed the two men, and tell the police to warn other women about those two blackguards!"

He spoke sharply, with authority, but when he turned his attention back to me, his voice was gentle, and his clasp on my arm light, as he said.

"Come, my dear. We shall take you home now. If the police wish to ask you any more questions, they can do so in the morning."

Jane and Max were in the villa when we arrived there. They were both deeply shocked when they heard what had happened, but after her initial gasps of dismay, Jane took me in hand.

"Melissa," she shooed me upstairs to my room. "I shall run hot water into the bath for you. A long soak will help to relax you both mentally and physically," she followed in my wake. "Once you are in bed," she continued, "I shall bring you a drink of hot chocolate—much better for you than brandy, in this instance, I think."

She disappeared into the bathroom, and from my room, as I wearily stripped off my ruined dress, I could hear the splash of water filling the tub, and could smell the fragrance of the pine crystals Jane was adding to it.

By the time I had bathed and dried myself, and

116

returned to my room, Carlo and Jake, supervised by Jane, were pushing a single divan bed into the corner between the window and the wardrobe, while Max stood looking on, clutching pillows and bed covers.

"You are not going to be allowed to sleep alone tonight," said Jane firmly. "I am going to keep an eye on you!"

"I'll be all right!" I protested. "Please don't put yourself to so much trouble for me."

"My dear child!" Jane gave me a hug. "It's no trouble! I am delighted to be able to do something for you in return for the way you looked after Leo and Jake when they had that accident in their final year at the university."

She urged the men from the room, so that I could take off my bathrobe and put on the pale blue cotton nightie, with the demurely high Victorian neckline edged with white lace, which she had laid out on the bed for me.

"I shall go and fetch the chocolate for you," she said, following the men to the door and telling them, "and you can say 'Goodnight' to Melissa now! She isn't to be bothered with any more questions tonight!"

She sounded so like me when, as assistant matron in the Château I had fussed over my girls in sick bay like a mother hen, that I found myself smiling for the first time for a couple of hours!

Dear Jane, I thought, as she closed the door behind her, and I put on my nightie and slipped into bed. You are kind and you are nice and you are so very competent, even if you can't cook, that you will make some lucky man a good wife some day—

The smile faded from my face when I remembered that that some day was going to be soon, and that the lucky man was going to be Jake.

I pushed my face against the pillow, to try to keep back the tears that pricked at my eyelids, when I recalled how only half an hour ago, Jake had held me tight in his arms, and stroked my hair, and I had felt so safe, yes, so happy with him, in spite of what had happened. For me, I thought desolately, there could be no happy marriage, because for me, there would never be any one to compare with my uncle's god-son.

I slept intermittently that night, in spite of the soothing hot drink Jane had given me, and in spite of the reassuring sound of her deep breathing from the near-by divan.

Strange images flitted through my mind. A hotch potch of faces appeared in my dreams, coming closer and closer in menace, then dissolving into a red nothingness as I tried to identify them. The apparition which drifted most often through my nightmarish visions was a creature, now like a huge black bat with its wings extended, now white as a shapeless ghost enveloped in a shroud, which came closer and closer, with invisible hands holding a scarf, ready to wind it around my neck, like a noose.

I tossed and turned restlessly, trying to rid my mind of these images, but the sky was paling to dawn before I eventually fell into a sound, dreamless slumber from which I was awakened some hours later by the same sounds which wakened me the previous morning—the cheerful clatter of plates from the kitchen, and the murmur of voices from the patio.

I glanced across at Jane's bed. It was tidily made up, and before leaving the room, she had opened the bedroom window to let in the sunny warmth of the new day.

Feeling surprisingly wide-awake I got out of bed, took a hasty shower, and dressing myself in fresh pink denims and a pink shirt, I hurried down the stairs and out to the courtyard, where the other members of the household were sitting around the trestle table, already enjoying breakfast.

They looked up with surprise as I came through the french windows to join them.

"Melissa!" exclaimed Jane. "We were going to let you have a long sleep! How do you feel?" she asked solicitously.

"Very wide awake!" I smiled at the faces turned toward me, "and," I added, wrinkling my nose in appreciation of the smell of freshly brewed coffee and oven hot crusty rolls, "extremely hungry!"

"That's Melissa for you!" Jake grinned. "There is no one quite like her," his voice seemed to soften. "It does not matter what happens, she never loses her appetite for food!"

I sat down in the vacant chair between Max and Leo, while Jane poured coffee into a cup and handed it to me, saying, "Are you quite sure you feel all right?"

"You had a very nasty experience," said Max.

"Yes, but Jake rescued me in the nick of time— like one of the old Pearl White dramas!" I said lightly, hoping that they would change the subject. I did not want to be reminded of what had almost happened in the dark alley.

However, I was not to be allowed to forget the episode. We had scarcely finished breakfast when Carlo arrived with his policeman brother-in-law, who was wanting to ask me more about the incident.

I told him I had already told Carlo all about it, but the policeman was hopeful that he might be able to jog my memory into recalling something about the men which would help in their identification, something which I might have overlooked in the state I had been in immediately after the event.

"We have asked the commanders of the ships whose men were on shore leave, if we can hold an identity parade," he said. "They are prepared to give their consent, but," he continued, "we do not wish to go to this trouble if you do not think you could pick the men out."

Leo and Jake retreated from the patio, along with Max and Jane, when the police captain sat down at the table to question me, but Carlo stayed on, and thoughtfully poured out a fresh cup of coffee for me.

"Come, Melissa," he smiled at me encouragingly as I took the cup from him. "Try to think back to last night, from the moment the conga started. Take your time about it," he put his hand on my shoulder. "It is often quite amazing what the eyes see, without being aware of what they note at the time."

Jane, thoughtful as ever, appeared with two extra cups, and more coffee, and retreated once more into the house, although to my surprise Carlo still remained at the table, as if he intended to sit through what I thought was supposed to be an official police interrogation.

He sensed my surprise, and explained, as he poured out coffee for himself and his brother-in-law.

"I am not presuming on my relationship with the Captain by staying with you, Melissa. I am here," he smiled reassuringly, "because in my job I am used to extracting information from people, and Patrizio thinks I may be able to help him, especially if there are any language difficulties," he referred to his brother-in-law's inadequate English and to the fact that my Italian, while adequate for most occasions, might not be up to the mark when it came to answering the type of questions the policeman might have to ask me.

I cupped my hands round the coffee cup and nodded. "I understand Carlo, and I am also glad that you can stay," I added. "Your presence makes me feel less nervous."

The police captain lit a cigarette, and after sitting back to watch the spiral of blue smoke which he exhaled drift up to the vine covered trellis he said softly.

"Bene, Signorina Gilchrist. Now, tell me slowly, what took place from the moment you and Mr. Carnegie and Carlo here, joined in with the others to dance the conga."

I closed my eyes, to try and review the scene, but for seconds I could think of nothing at all, although my senses seemed more aware of what was going on around me at the moment than usual.

I heard the suck of breath as the policeman inhaled his cigarette, and Carlo's slow breathing from the chair next to mine. I could hear the rasping of a cicada in the vines above my head, and the ebb and flow of the waves against the rocks which lay below the cliffs at the end of the garden and the distant whine of an airplane's engines as it came in over the sea toward the airport at Fertilia. I could hear the distant growling of the guard dogs from the Villa Magnolia, and the everyday noises from the house behind us—dishes clattering, the subdued murmur of voices, the rattle of a typewriter, and almost unaware that the memory had come to me, or that I had spoken aloud, I murmured.

"The most frightening thing about the episode was the silence!" I set my coffee cup on the table as my hand trembled at the thought, sending the liquid spilling over the edge. "The men never spoke to me, or to each other! They were so quiet! So frighteningly quiet! I don't think I would have been so terrified if they had threatened me with words, or gloated with laughter—"

Quietly, not wishing to stem the flow of returning memory, Carlo put a napkin into my coffee wet hands, and as I dried them automatically, I stared ahead of me, my eyes opened now, but not seeing the blueness of the sea and sky which stretched to unite in the distant horizon, not seeing the brilliance of the roses and the hibiscus in the garden in front of me, seeing, instead, the reflection of the blue lights from the enclosed fish ponds in the Mermaid Cave on the white uniforms of the sailors who had pushed their way onto the dance floor, feeling once again the pressure of the hands on my waist, pushing me firmly after the man who had joined the conga ahead of me, recalling my moment of disquiet when we had broken away from the main head, in the dim-lit courtyard, my desire to wriggle away from the dance and return to my table, mingled with impatience for myself at being a spoil sport, for not wanting to keep up with the gay dancers who swayed in and out of the candle-lit tables, in and out the pillars of the vine covered portico which led to the back gate.

My fingers tightened on the damp napkin as the succeeding moments flashed into my mind, those moments when the leader had opened the postern gate and we had jogged into the lane, so deeply dark from the shadows of the overhanging houses, and when I had been pushed roughly forward by the man who was dancing behind me, and in stumbling forward, had realized that I was alone in that lane, with two drunken sailors!

The memory was now quite vivid, as if a camera bulb had flashed, revealing the scene.

"One of the men was tallish, Carlo!" I exclaimed. "About your height!"

"His face!" asked the policeman. "Did you get a look at his face?"

Memory faltered.

"I remember his teeth!" I frowned in concentration. "They seemed very white, very even. His mouth was open in a horrible snarl—but his face—" I shook my head. "No—the alley was not lit at that part, and the houses cast dark, moon shadows."

"How about the other man?" prompted Carlo.

"The one who led me to the alley?" I faltered. "It is the tall one, who threatened me with the scarf, who sticks in my mind."

I closed my eyes again, forcing the scene to reappear on the screen of my mind.

"The other man," I repeated slowly, "yes! yes! Now I do remember something about him! He wasn't very tall, not much bigger than me, as a matter of fact, and he had fair hair! Yes! I remember the fair hair! And I am almost sure that he had some kind of beard!" I turned to look at the two men. "But that is all, I think."

"Bene," breathed the police captain. "That should be a help in identifying him!" he looked at me hopefully. "Are you sure there is nothing else?"

I hesitated. "He had long nails. I felt them dig into me as I wrenched away from him, and they caught on my dress, and ripped it, but that is all!" I pressed my fingers against my eyes. "Nothing else about them comes to mind."

"I think you have done very well," said Carlo approvingly, and pushed back his chair.

His brother-in-law squashed out the stub of his cigarette in the ash tray.

"Si! Grazie, Signorina Gilchrist!" he stood up. "Now I can give the naval commanders a fairly distinctive description of one of the men. No, no!" he added as I made to rise. "I shall see myself out, and leave you to finish your breakfast in peace.

"Buon appetito!" he gave a small bow, and followed by Carlo, walked smartly into the house, leaving me sitting at the table alone with the dregs of the unpleasant memories he had stirred up.

THIRTEEN

I remained seated at the breakfast table until the slamming of a car door and the revving of an engine indicated that the Police Captain was on his way back to the Questura to make use of the further information I had given him, before I hurried into the house and went upstairs to the bathroom to wash my hands on which the spilt coffee had dried stickily, and to splash cold water over my face, which felt equally hot and sticky after the trying interview.

I decided not to think about the possible identity parade at which I would be called upon to try to pick out the guilty men. I wanted to put last night's unpleasant incident out of my mind, and keep my thoughts from the brutish men who had selected a random victim for their savage amusement.

I wanted to think only of pleasant things; of the sun shining from the cloudless sky; of the beauty of the shrubs, heavy with blossom, which brightened the garden; and of the blue, blue sea, which looked so tempting to swim in as it lapped the sands of the cove below.

I knew that Jake and Leo were as fond of swimming as I was, and they had mentioned that it was safe to bathe in the cove. I decided to try to persuade them to go with me now, down the cliff path to the sandy little bay, so that we could enjoy a swim together, and dive from the rocks, and even do some underwater swimming, for I had noticed snorkels on the stand in the hall.

Yes, I decided enthusiastically, a swim was exactly what I was in need of at the moment, to help me forget the past unpleasantness, and to remind me that life was good, and that there were more pleasant people in the world than there were mean and wicked ones.

To my surprise, Carlo Roncardi had not gone off with his brother-in-law, but had joined Jake and the others in the kitchen, where he was sitting on one of the high stools, chatting to Jane as she washed the breakfast dishes, while Jake dried them and Leo stacked them away.

I entered the kitchen as Max was emerging from the doorway which led down to the cellar below the house, carrying a box full of beer bottles. He dumped his burden on the floor and disappeared from view into the cellar once more, calling,

"How many bottles of wine do you think we shall need, Carlo?"

"I'll leave that to your judgement, Max," he replied, slipping off the stool and lifting the box of beer up to place it on the kitchen table.

Jane looked round, and saw me standing in the doorway.

"There you are, Melissa! Good! You can help pack the glasses!"

"And be sure to put a can opener and a corkscrew in the box with them," said Max, reappearing, and looking across at Jane as he added, "There, my dear! I remembered about them this time!"

Jane laughed and retorted lightly. "That makes a change!"

I looked at them all in bewilderment.

"What glasses are you talking about?"

"You will get them over there, in that cupboard," Jane nodded directions to me. "We won't use the good ones."

"I'll get them for you, Melissa," Jake draped the dish towel over a towel rod. "You won't be able to reach them," he sauntered across the room, "they are on the top shelf."

"What do we want with glasses at this time of day?" I asked in bewilderment. "We have only just finished breakfast!"

Jane looked at me in surprise. "Had you forgotten, Melissa? This is the day of the picnic to Lake Baratz! Carlo's sister is providing the food, remember, and we were asked to bring the drinks."

"Oh!" I shook my head. "I had forgotten," I frowned.

"Don't you like picnics, Melissa?" Carlo raised his dark brows in query.

"She used to love them," Jake answered for me, "but perhaps after teaching all this 'Savoir-Vivre and Etiquette' nonsense, she may feel they are rather infra dig?" he teased me.

"No! It's not that!" I looked at Carlo. "I thought that perhaps your brother-in-law might want to see me again today—about the identity parade he mentioned."

"No, no! You need not worry about that, Melissa, cara," he said gently. "Such things take time to organize, especially in the present circumstances. Moreover, there would only be the need for a parade, if they find a sailor with fair hair and a beard, answering to your description."

"That's right!" I said, perking up. "So I don't need to stay at home after all?"

"Of course not!" he assured me.

"Good! As Jake says, I love picnics, especially if the weather is fair, and we don't have to sizzle sausages over a rain-washed fire!"

"I have asked my island gods for a day of sunshine for you," Carlo twinkled at me. "Even Sardinia does not look beautiful in the rain!"

The men carried the hamper of bottles out to the Rover, which, being much larger than Jake's little Fiat, was going to be pressed into service for the picnic.

The capacious trunk easily held the hampers, the camp chairs, the rugs, the bathing costumes and towels and all the other paraphernalia for the day's outing.

Jake went back to the house when we had finished packing in the stuff, to make sure that the windows and doors were securely locked and bolted, and that the shutters had been closed to keep the house cool, and Max eased himself in behind the steering wheel. Although he did not particularly like driving on the island, he would not let anyone else drive his elderly car in case they harmed it!

Jane slipped into the passenger seat beside him, but as I was about to get into the back seat with Leo, Carlo caught my arm.

"You come with me in my car, Melissa," he insisted. "That way, I can point at all the places of interest along our route."

Jake, returning from his tour of safety inspection, gave Carlo a sharp look when he heard this invitation, but I was glad of the excuse not to sit in the Rover, between Leo and Jake, and looking at Carlo with a smile, I accepted his offer.

Max started the Rover, and Carlo and I stood to one side as the car moved slowly down the driveway, then strolled after it, to where Carlo's dashing looking scarlet Alfa Romeo sports car was parked outside on the road.

"Where does your sister live?" I asked Carlo as we trailed sedately behind Max's Rover through the streets of Alghero.

"She lives in the new part of the town," he told me. "However, we are not meeting her at her house. I thought it better to arrange to meet at our usual picnic spot by the lake."

He fumbled for his sunglasses on the shelf under the dashboard, and put them on. I glanced sideways at him, and decided that he looked very suave and sophisticated and attractive, with his snow white, open-necked shirt, bright against the almost mahogany tan of his skin, the silk, scarlet cravat neatly tucked into the V-line, his patrician features, and the almost negligent way his smooth, brown, long fingered hands, with a broad gold signet ring set with a small diamond sparkling on his ring finger, rested on the steering wheel.

When we had passed the railway station, following the same road on which Jake had taken me the previous day on our visit to the nuraghe, instead of continuing to tail behind Max, Carlo unexpectedly turned off to the right, into a narrow dirt track road, which led through a field of sweet corn.

For a second I felt apprehensive, and the moment of tension must have shown on my face, for Carlo turned to me, with a smile, and even through the smoky lens of his glasses I could see the twinkle in his eyes as he remarked.

"It is all right, Melissa! I am not a bandit about to kidnap a lovely young hostage! A friend of mine has a little farm near here, and I want to buy some fresh fruit for our picnic from him."

The fields of sweet corn gave way to orchards on either side of the track. Peaches and apricots hung from the trees like glowing lanterns among the dark green leaves, and there were pears too, and apples.

"Later there will be pomegranates," said Carlo. "On those trees over there, where there are still pink flowers showing."

"Pomegranates!" I exclaimed. "I have never seen pomegranates growing before!" I turned to stare at the trees, on which I could now see the shape of the unripe fruit.

"Perhaps they will be ripe before you leave the island, Melissa," he said. "In that case, you will be able to pull some from the trees!"

"Somehow I did not imagine Sardinia would be like this!" I stared around me at the acres of fruit trees as we got out of the car beside a small, white-washed house near to which hens were scraping in the dust of the yard, and a dog, tied to a pole, opened one wary eye to assess if we were friends or foes. "I imagined it would be more arid," I went on, "with less vegetation, and more sand and scree."

"Inland, it can be like that," he nodded, "but you should see the island in springtime, my dear. That is when it is most beautiful. The orchards are drifts of the white blossom of pear trees and the pink blossom of peach and almond; the fields are lilac with cyclamen, and rock roses cover the scree, while our tall asphodels wave in the wind!"

"Asphodels grow here?" I asked.

"But of course! The asphodel is our island flower. The Herba Sardonica!"

"The Herba Sardonica?" I repeated.

"You must have heard of a sardonic smile, surely?"

I nodded.

"Well, the name derives from this plant, which the ancients credited with poisonous qualities. It tastes more bitter than gall, and contorts the face into a grimace. It is said to induce moods of frenetic gaiety, and wild laughter—"

"I am glad you told me!" I said to him. "I always wondered about the expression—a sardonic smile."

"Fortunately there are more cheerful tales about the island's gods and goddesses," he said. "I must tell you some of them, one day."

I looked at him curiously.

"You love your homeland, don't you?"

He nodded. "Yes, Melissa. It is beautiful and wild and it can be cruel, especially in the interior, where much has still to be done to improve conditions, and where like the wild land they inhabit,

133

the people, the clans, I think you would call them, are also wild and can be cruel—"

"You are talking of the bandit country?" I asked.

He nodded, as he rapped on the door of the little house. "Yes, the interior is a land that used to breed bandits, although now we are doing our best to bring more aids to civilization to the people there."

At his knocking, the dog stood up and barked and made a dash toward us, snapping wildly, but fortunately the rope which held it kept it out of our reach.

"Verdi must be out working in one of his other orchards," Carlo frowned when there was no reply to his knock. "Still," he took hold of my arm, and guided me away from the dog, "we can help ourselves to fruit. I shall leave a note to tell my friend that we called."

He let go of my arm, took his diary from his pocket, tore out a page and scribbled something on it. Then, carefully keeping out of the range of the snapping dog, he went round to the back of the house and pushed the note under the door, saying as he did so.

"Verdi would not have found it if I had pushed it under the front door. That one is only opened when visitors call!"

We took a basket which hung on a pole at the end of one of the rows of fruit trees, filled it with a variety of fruit, and returned to the car.

We drove along another dirt track, which rejoined the main road beside a cluster of houses, a wine co-operative, Carlo told me, and as we turned the corner, we were in time to see Max's Rover disappear round the bend a quarter of a mile ahead of us.

We followed Max's car from this point on for about a couple of miles along the highway, until we turned off to a sandy track which led between pine woods, and across the almost dried up bed of a small stream, down to the sloping, sandy shores of a lake, which according to Carlo, was the only natural fresh water lake on the island.

Ahead of us, Max had drawn the Rover up alongside a large Fiat, and we in turn stopped alongside his car, to be surrounded, almost before we had set foot on the ground, by a group of excited children, who grabbed at Carlo's hand, wanting to show him without delay the castles they had already built in the sand.

I was introduced to the youngsters, two boys of eight and ten and their young sister who was only six, and then I met Carlo's sister, Magdalena, tall and dark and good-looking as Carlo, and her husband, Tomaso Ponti, who was a lawyer.

I helped Jane and Magdalena to set out the tables and chairs and the food for the picnic, while Leo took the beer down to the lake and put the bottles in the water to keep them cool.

Jake and Max, joined by Tomaso, went off to play football with the boys on a grassy patch near the edge of the pine wood, but Carlo lazily squatted down on a flat stone beside a pipe line which led out into the lake, broke a biscuit into small pieces and flung the crumbs to the small birds which quickly congregated around him.

When the tables had been set up, and the fire

of twigs and driftwood which the children had earlier collected were lit, to sizzle sausages over, Jane and Magdalena and I went across to watch the football match.

Max, looking as unlike a forty-five year old professor as was possible, was acting as referee in the two a side match between the boys and the men, and he was in his element, dashing around, whistling and unfairly encouraging the youngsters in their winning tactics against Tomaso and Jake.

"Max should have married years ago," I turned to Jane. "He has always had a wonderful way with children and would have made a super father."

Magdalena chuckled.

"He is enjoying himself, isn't he? I am afraid poor Tomaso is out of training."

"It's all your rich cooking that is to blame for that!" Carlo came over and slipped an arm around his sister's shoulder. "You should tell him to take more exercise!"

"I am going to tell him that lunch is ready!" she laughed at her brother. "We are not all such physical fitness fanatics as you are, Carlo!"

If the picnic meal Magdalena had provided measured up to their usual fare, it was no wonder that Thomas was so plump and cheerful, I thought as I licked my fingers after enjoying a plateful heaped with various cold meats and chicken legs.

"This is the life for me!" Jake sighed, emptying the last drop from a bottle of lake-chilled beer down his throat. "Sunshine, good food, cold beer, and a lazy afternoon ahead!"

He stretched himself out on the sandy shore,

and Jane expertly pushed a towel under his head to add to his comfort.

It was the only personal gesture I had seen pass between the two. Truth to tell, in spite of knowing what I did about them, it was difficult to imagine them as lovers. Friends, yes, but that was all. On the other hand with either Leo or Max always around, they could have decided to be extremely circumspect, so that there was no chance of these two in particular guessing at their relationship.

Jake closed his eyes, and Leo, following his example, pulled off his shirt and stretched himself out to sunbathe. Max and Tomaso helped the children build a more ornate sand castle by the water's edge, digging a channel down to the lake for the water to run up it to form a moat.

I was sitting on the grassy bank indulging in girl talk with Jane and Magdalena, but Carlo came over to us, and looking down at me said,

"If the others want to be lazy, Melissa, let them. But you come with me," he held out his hands to pull me to my feet. "I want to show you the place from which, when the level of the lake is low, they say you can see the old drowned city that lies beneath its waters, and we might even walk along to the cliff top, where you will see Porto Ferro, one of the loveliest bays in the area. After that," he went on, as I held my hands up to his and let him help me to my feet, "we might even walk to the foot of Monte Forte, over there—"

"Don't let Carlo walk you off your feet, Melissa," grunted Leo. "He thinks a ten mile trek is a gentle stroll!"

"And don't take my girl off into the wilds, where we can't keep an eye on you!" Jake opened one eye and squinted up at us. "We thought you had kidnapped her, when you dropped out of sight on our way here!"

Carlo laughed.

"Melissa will be quite safe with me!" he assured them. "Come, cara," he took me by the arm, and we sauntered off, along the shore of the lake, into another small pine wood, which was full of bird song, and out onto a deeply rutted, serpentine path, which led uphill in one direction, and towards the coast in the other.

"That path there," Carlo indicated the uphill one, "eventually leads to the Pink Grotto, on the far side of the bay. Some other time I shall take you there, but not today. I do not want the children to ask about it. When they are older, I shall tell them its whereabouts, but it is not a safe place for children to wander in. The pool in the cave is said to be bottomless, and there are dangerous undertows in the water."

"The Pink Grotto?" I repeated the name with a puzzled look. "I am sure I heard the name mentioned recently, but I thought it was a café or a night club, or something like that."

Carlo laughed. "My Pink Grotto is no night club! It is one of the island's many wonders, like the Grotto of Neptune and the Elephant Rock, except that it has not been popularized as the others have been, and in fact, very few people know of its existence, for it does not appear in any guide book or on any map of the area."

"The Pink Grotto!" I repeated the name. "I wish I could remember where I heard about it. It is strange, but I associate it with Sardinia somehow."

Carlo looked puzzled. "Jake or Max might have mentioned it," he frowned, "but I do not know where they could have learned of its existence. I have not spoken of it to them, but of course, in their researches of the island, they could have come across some tale about it, for centuries ago, because of its two entrances, it was used as a hideout by the Barbary pirates."

"If you are so keen to keep its whereabouts a secret," I smiled at him, "why have you told me about it?"

"Apart from its history, and the secret entrance from the cliffs, it is very beautiful, Melissa. The pink rocks make even the water seem pink, and their formations are like fairy palaces. It is a romantic spot to linger with a pretty girl," he grinned. "Molto romantico!"

He smiled down at me, and looking up into his handsome face, his gay, flirtative eyes, a memory surfaced only to vanish before I could retain it, and I had the feeling that there was an association between Carlo, or someone like Carlo, and the Pink Grotto.

Someone like Carlo! Yes, that was the key! Now I remembered!

"There must be a night club in Milan of that name!" I said trimuphantly. "It was at the Milan airport, when I was waiting for the plane to Alghero, that I heard it mentioned! A man was making an

139

assignation with a woman to meet him there! I even remember the date," I smiled. "It was the 7th of this month!"

I shook my head. "Isn't it ridiculous how an unimportant conversation, which had nothing at all to do with me, should stay in my mind!" I said, "And yet I can remember so little about the drunken sailors who attacked me last night!"

"That is because the mind automatically tries to reject the unpleasant," replied Carlo, as he pulled aside the branch of a small tree, to let me pass along the path, which grew narrower and narrower.

Because we had to walk single file, and since he was behind me, I did not notice the strange expression which crossed his face at my words.

FOURTEEN

I enjoyed my walk with Carlo. He was interested in wild life as I was, and he told me the names of plants which were new to me, both in Italian and English, the names of the wild birds we saw, and the names of the surrounding hills and the little coves and inlets along the rugged shore, which were all clearly visible from the vantage point to which we had climbed.

The air was balmy, and heavy with the sweet scent of myrtle and the other aromatic herbs which covered the hard and stony ground of the shelving land above the clifftops. Here and there, where the ground was less stony, wild flowers grew. There were the usual pink and yellow thistles and trailing bindweed, orange crepis and yellow euphorbia, but when I exclaimed with pleasure at finding a clump of pure white marguerites, Carlo smiled and gallantly stooped to gather me a bouquet of them.

"My mother called these moon daisies," he said softly. "A pretty name for a pretty flower to give to a pretty girl!" his fingers touched mine as he handed me the bouquet, and I found the contact pleasant, would have yielded to the pleasure, if I had been heart whole and fancy free, for Carlo was fun to be with, and a flirtation with him would have been a gay and light-hearted affair, but I was not heart whole, and my fancy was a prisoner of a man who could not be mine; a man for whom I pined; the one love of my life.

Slowly I took the flowers from my companion and buried my face in their soft petals, so that he might not see the sadness which had come into my eyes.

"I think it is high time we were on our way back to rejoin the others!" Carlo's voice was harsh. "They will be wondering what we have been up to!"

"They will all be too preoccupied with their own affairs to worry about us!" I retorted.

"What about Jake? He is not going to be pleased at my monopolizing his girl!"

"Jake's girl?" I managed a derisive laugh. "I am not Jake's girl! What gave you that idea?"

Carlo shot me a puzzled look. "I have known Jake for a number of years, and he has always talked a lot about you."

I shrugged. "I daresay he has—as a man talks to his friends about his sister—as you would have talked to Jake about your sisters. That is the be all and end all of our relationship!"

"But you are not his sister!" persisted Carlo. "You are a very attractive young woman, whom he admires!"

I shook my head. "He has always looked upon me as the sister he never had, and he has been like another brother to me, an additional member of our family!" I tried to keep emotion from my voice, although there was asperity in my tone as I added.

142

"Surely, Carlo, with your knowledge of human psychology, you have noticed that it is Jane Jake finds most attractive. Jane," I repeated. "I would not be at all surprised if he married her one day!"

Carlo's eyes narrowed. "So?" he looked at me. "Is that how the wind blows? I thought—"

"Then you thought wrongly," I interrupted him crisply. "In any case, let's forget this conversation, shall we?" I added, realizing that I had inadvertently betrayed Jane's secret. "I could be wrong about Jake and Jane."

"Yes!" he agreed. "You could be!" I thought I detected a hint of amusement in his tone, as he repeated, "You could be!"

When we came to the clearing beside the lake where the rest of the picnic party was still lounging, Jake looked up. At this precise moment Carlo lightly lifted me up in his arms to carry me over a broken tree branch which lay across our path.

"Where did you get to?" asked Leo. "We were beginning to think you had got lost!"

"We were gathering moon daisies!" I said lightly as Carlo set me back on my feet.

"They are the right flowers for Melissa, aren't they?" said Carlo. "Large-eyed, innocent looking—"

"Don't let Carlo lead you on, Melissa," Jake said gruffly. "He has a different line for every girl he takes out!"

"Now you are spoiling my chances with Melissa!" Carlo chaffed him. "That is not fair, is it?" he appealed to the others.

"Behave yourself, Carlo!" Magdalena admonished him. "It is not right—" she stopped in mid-sentence as a spattering of heavy raindrops

143

ricocheted off the ground, and almost simultaneously a crash of thunder reverberated among the hills surrounding us.

"Mamma mia!" she exclaimed, scrambling to her feet. "Quick, children! Get your things into the car. Tomaso! The hamper!"

We all grabbed at whatever was nearest to us, and ran to stuff our gear in the car trunks, and get under cover in the cars ourselves, before the storm broke with violent fury over the lake.

Lightning flashed startlingly close, and the rumble of thunder shook the Rover into which Jake had bundled me. I looked out at the view, which was distorted by the rain streaming down the windows.

The lake had been whipped into a sea of high, foam flecked waves by the gale which had sprung up so suddenly. Great pools of water were forming on the patch of grass where the men had been playing football with Tomaso's boys, and the track we had walked along was like a small stream.

"We'll have to get on our way, or we shall be bogged down!" Jake shouted to Max, his voice made almost inaudible by the crackle of thunder.

Tomaso had already set off down the trail, and a hoot from Carlo's car indicated that we were to go next, and that he would bring up the rear.

At times the car wheels skidded in the soft mud of deep potholes which the streaming water covered over, and at other times, the swaying branches of the pine trees, bending over before the storm, brushed against the roof of the car and against the windshield, almost pulling the wipers off. It was a relief to get on to the hard-surfaced main road, although it too was awash with water.

The storm passed, but a drizzle of rain persisted until the time we came to Alghero, where with a tooting of his car horn to say goodbye, Tomaso left the convoy to turn into the Via Sassari to head for his own home. In due turn, Carlo, with a flash of his headlights bidding us farewell, left us near the Piazza Sulis, and we continued on our way to the Villa Gelsomino on our own.

At the villa, the garden bore testimony to the wildness of the tempest, for the flowers lay drooping and mud-spattered, and the pink and white petals of the oleanders floated in puddles which had formed on the path below the eaves of the house.

"Even in Sardinia, a picnic can end in rain!" Jane remarked as we unpacked the chairs and the rest of the paraphernalia from the car. "Still, it is nice to be home early. We can have a cold meal in the living room, and watch TV at the same time," she suggested.

"Nothing too highbrow!" she added, noting the expression on my face. "Truth to tell, I did not wish to miss the first episode of the new 'Avengers' series!"

We spent a pleasant, relaxed evening, and got to bed early, with the result that I woke shortly after six the following morning, feeling completely rested, but very restless!

I got out of bed and crossed over to the window and opened the shutters. Sunlight came flooding warmly into the room, and already the heat from its rays had dried up last night's puddles in the garden, and revived the stricken blooms, which were standing erect again, and perkily turning their lovely faces to the sky.

I stepped out onto the balcony. Not a single cloud marred the blue of the heavens, and beyond the cliff tops, the sea was an even deeper blue.

Today was the day my work as cook at the Villa Gelsomino officially started, I reminded myself. Max had told me that breakfast was at eight o'clock, to give them time to arrive at their dig by nine. They had chosen not to set up camp near the site, because of the wildness of the area, which was in the heart of the "bandit" country. Carlo, in fact, had advised against it, saying that while local vendettas rarely affected outsiders, there was no point in taking any chances, especially when there was a woman in the team.

Breakfast of rolls, fruit and coffee, with boiled eggs for the men, would take no time at all to prepare, and I was wondering if I would manage to get down to the cove for a quick bathe before I set the table, when I noticed a man step out onto the patio below me.

Instinctively I stepped back into my room. At the same moment, Jake called softly up to me. "Are you there, Melissa? I thought I heard you open your shutters."

I stepped back on the narrow balcony and leaned over the rail.

"Jake, are you game for a swim before breakfast?" I asked.

"Just what I was going to ask you!" He smiled up at me. "Take sneakers with you," he added. "There are stony patches in the cove."

"Shall I put on my swim suit here, or change at the foot of the cliffs?" I asked.

"It doesn't matter—although I would advise you to take a robe or something like that to wear for the climb down and back. It is quite a scramble down the cliff path, and you need some kind of protection against grazing your arms and knees—in fact—" he suggested, "we could go by car to the cove. Yes. That's what we'll do. Hurry and dress, my love, and I shall meet you at the car in three minutes!"

I hurried back into my room, put on the low-backed, beautifully cut swim suit which I had bought in Florence at Christmas time, buttoned the matching blue robe over it, tied my hair back from my face with the terry cloth alice band which went with the set, and cramming a comb, sun cream, a dry costume and sunglasses into my beach bag, I crept softly from my room and went to join Jake.

"That was quick," he said approvingly. "And have I ever told you that you should always wear blue? It suits you," he smiled, as he put the car into gear, and we moved slowly forward down the drive, the grit crunching beneath the tires as we set off for the short ride along the coast road, to the path which led down to the cove—a path which was so overgrown with grass and wild flowers, that it would not have been recognized as such at a casual glance.

"This is much easier, and certainly much quicker, than scrambling down the tortuous path from the garden," said Jake. "Mark you," he added, "it isn't exactly the best treatment for car springs!"

The cove was small, semi-circled by high cliffs and the boulders which had crashed from the over-hanging rocks.

Jake discreetly retreated behind one of the boulders to change into the scarlet trunks which he had retrieved from the back seat of the car along with a pair of beach shoes. I unbuttoned my dress in the car, tucked my hair under a well fitting rubber cap, and gingerly made my way across the rocky shore to the sandy patch at the water's edge.

I put one foot tentatively in the waves, and withdrew it very quickly, for the water seemed icy.

"Don't dither!" shouted Jake, as he scrambled over the rocks, to get to one which overhung a deep pool. "Come on! I shall race you to the other side!" he plunged into the water as I waded slowly out into the waves, to take off in the direction in which he had pointed.

In seconds I was enjoying myself. The initial sensation of chill had vanished, and the sea felt buoyant and quite warm as I followed Jake at a leisurely pace across the bay.

"Come on, Melissa! You can do better than that!" he teased me as he gave me a helping hand to pull me up to the rock where he had scrambled up several seconds ahead of me.

"I am not in a competitive mood this morning, Jake," I said, lying on the smooth stone to sun myself.

"That is one way of saying you know you will never get the better of me, so why try?" Jake grinned at me, and teasingly trickled sand which he had scooped up from a hollow in the rock, between my shoulder blades.

"Stop that, Jake!" I said crossly, rolling away from him and almost sliding back into the water as I did so.

Jake had no right to be here, alone with me, looking at me like this.

"What is wrong with you Melissa?" he asked, puzzled. "You have been as prickly as a cactus these past few days." He shook his head. "It isn't like you!"

He put out his hand and touched my shoulder. "Don't let these incidents which have happened to you get you down, my dear. Try to put them out of your mind."

"We should have asked Leo and Jane to join us here," I sat up and stared morosely at the distant horizon. "What on earth will they think of us, going off and leaving them. And Max too, for that matter," I added as an afterthought.

Jake laughed.

"Leo doesn't believe in getting out of bed until the last possible minute in the morning. Max isn't all that fond of swimming, as you know, and as for Jane," he smiled and shook his head. "Well, Jane's a pretty wonderful person, but she does have her weaknesses, like her inability to cook, as you have already been told, and swimming in the open sea is something which she loathes!

"She cannot stand the thought of being in the company of wriggly fishes like these, look!" he pointed down into the water, in whose clear depths I could see a myriad of small fish darting about. "She maintains that it is much more civilized to swim in a man-made pool, where there is no natural wild life ready to nibble at your toes!"

"I don't believe it!" I shook my head. "You are trying to pull my leg, Jake. I am sure Jane is not the type to be upset by creepy, crawly fishy things, like Sally."

"You don't know her as well as I do," he informed me, standing up. "Come on, Melissa. We have been here long enough! If you don't want to get fired on your first day at work, it is time we were getting back."

We dived one after the other into the sea, and raced for the shore. This time, Jake only won by a stroke.

We dried ourselves quickly and went back to the villa, where I hurriedly changed into my usual denim and matching shirt uniform, and went downstairs again to set the breakfast table and prepare the meal.

We had scarcely had time to finish our first cup of coffee when Carlo Roncardi came wandering around the side of the house and mounted the steps leading to the patio.

I was as surprised to see him as the others, and although we all returned his cheerful "Ciào" of greeting, I was anxious to know what had brought him to the villa at this early hour. Judging from the frown on Jake's face, I could see he was wondering the same thing.

"Carlo, I shall go and fetch you another cup," I said, rising and hurrying to the kitchen.

"We aren't on holiday any more, Carlo, you know," I heard Max say. "There is so much to be done at the site, and too little time at our disposal to do all that I want to do before returning to England, to take too much time off."

"I realize that, Professore," Carlo replied. "And I knew, too, that you were returning to work this morning. That is why I have called so early!"

Max gave him a worried look, and I felt a strange coldness sweep away from the warm pleasure I was still experiencing after my pleasant swim with Jake. Had Carlo come to bring more news about the sailors? Had he come, as an emissary from his brother-in-law, the police captain, to ask me, and the others too, who had been with me at the Mermaid Cave, to attend an identity parade to see if we could pick out the wanted men?

"Well?" queried Jake impatiently. "So you want to see us all about something? What is wrong?"

"I don't want to see all of you," replied Carlo slowly, and his eyes looked from Jane to me, and lingered, longest, on my face.

"Why did neither of you girls make mention of the accident in the Via Gilbert Ferret?" he addressed us both sharply. "Why did you not wait for the arrival of the police, to describe what happened?"

Jane and I both blushed.

"It—it wasn't anything to do with us!" Jane stammered. "We could not have helped the police in any way. We didn't see the man who crashed the motor bicycle, and—"

"And there were so many other witnesses," I interrupted her. "There didn't seem any point in our waiting. We honestly did not see exactly what happened."

"How did you know we were there, in any case?" queried Jane.

"Alghero is a small place, Signorina Hunter," there was stiff formality in Carlo's tone. "You have been living here for several weeks. As a stranger, you are naturally noticed by the locals, and noticed even more particularly because you are who you are—an assistant to the famous Professor Little, and also because you are tall for a woman, and very distinguished looking."

Jane flushed at his words.

"Yes," he went on. "You were recognized, and so were you," he looked at me. "You were described as a slim young girl, with a cap of gold hair and the complexion of a sun-kissed peach, by one of the young male witnesses," there was a hint of amusement in his tone as he added. "A very graphic description, wouldn't you say?"

I lowered my eyes, and blushed, as Jane had done.

"This witness also went on to say," Carlo's tone hardened, "that he had previously noticed the driver of the motorbike loitering in the roadway, and noticed him particularly because he thought the machine he was straddling was very like that of a colleague of his who works in the bank in the square. His reliability as a witness can be judged," Carlo added, "when I tell you that the machine he had noticed did belong to his colleague, and had been stolen from the parking place only minutes before the accident!"

"Yes," Carlo kept looking fixedly at me. "This young banker has proved an excellent witness, who said something else which interested the police a great deal, and which made my brother-in-law ask me if I would call on you this morning, as a friend—"

"What are you going on about, Carlo?" said Leo impatiently.

"Just this," Roncardi looked at the circle of interested faces. "This man said that it was not until the signorine came round the corner from the Via Carlo Alberto, that the man started up the engine, and went racing at speed down the road! He is of the opinion that the skid was caused deliberately, and that the driver, equally deliberately, before he jumped from the machine, steered it in the direction of Jane and Melissa!"

I gave a startled gasp. "That is ridiculous!"

Carlo ignored the interruption. He looked at me unblinkingly, then said, slowly.

"There have been three attempts on your life since you arrived here in Alghero, Melissa. So tell me, please, for your own sake, who would want to kill you? Who would like you out of the way? Who hates you so much, that he tries over and over again, to bring about your death?"

FIFTEEN

A stunned silence followed Carlo's dramatic pronouncement, a silence which was finally broken by an explosive remark from Jake.

"Poppycock!" he ejaculated. "Sheer and utter poppycock! Who on earth would want to kill Melissa?" he demanded angrily. "Carlo, you have become so obsessed with crime, that you see a criminal behind every action!"

Carlo paid no attention to Jake's outburst, but continued to look at me. "Well, Melissa," he repeated. "Have you any enemies? Is there someone you have hurt, however unwittingly? A lover? A jealous wife?"

"For goodness' sake, Carlo!" I exclaimed angrily. "How could I possibly have any enemies here, in Sardinia? I haven't been in the place a week! And as for your stupid talk of jealous wives and lovers," I went on furiously. "Can't you think of any other reasons for murder, than crimes of passion?"

"Most murders are crimes of passion," he said blandly, "although there are varying reasons for the passions!"

"Well, for your information, I don't have a lover. I am not in love with anyone, and no one is in love with me. Does that satisfy you?"

He gave me a long, speculative look, as if he didn't quite believe me, before he spoke again.

"Then, in that case, my brother-in-law will have to look elsewhere for a reason for these attempts on your life."

"Don't be silly!" I challenged him. "Haven't you ever heard of coincidences? I am quite sure the three incidents are unconnected! As far as the motor bicycle thief was concerned, when he skidded, he could have knocked down several people, and not just me, and as for the drunken sailors at the Mermaid Cave, they just happened to pick on me by accident. Any young girl would have done."

"Melissa is quite right," said Jane, backing me up. "You are trying to build a case on the sands of coincidence. If your brother-in-law wishes a statement from us as regards the incident in the Via Gilbert Ferret, then we shall be only too pleased to give him one, but for goodness sake don't think that what happened was anything other than a careless accident! The courts would be crowded with attempted murder cases if every time a car or a bike slipped and skidded, the driver was arrested on such a charge!"

"Poor Carlo!" Max intervened. "No one agrees with your theory, I am afraid, and if you knew Melissa as well as we do, you would know that she doesn't have an enemy in the world. She's not the type to make them!"

"There I would agree," Carlo conceded, and smiled at me. "Perhaps it is because I have never believed in a run of coincidences, that I am reading more into what has happened than I should."

Max glanced at his watch. "Carlo, if you don't want Jane to go with you, to see your brother-in-law, I would like to get on my way to work. I want to keep up with the schedule I have set for the day."

"And it is time we went to the airport to see if the spare part I ordered for our plane has arrived," said Jake. "I was promised it for this morning at the very latest. Coming Leo?"

Max and Jane went off together in the Rover to drive to their location near Torralba, where they would meet up with Mike and Stanley, who were going there direct from the house of the friends with whom they had been spending the weekend, and Jake and Leo went out to their car, to drive to the airport.

Although Carlo followed them down the drive to the road, where his scarlet Alfa Romeo was parked, and stood beside me, waving them good-bye, instead of driving off himself, and going about his own business, to my surprise, and somewhat to my consternation, he returned to the villa with me, saying, as he followed me into the house.

"Since there is nothing to report back to the questura, my work for the day is done!" he sat on the railing of the patio and plucked idly at the leaves of jasmine which trailed down from the overhead trellis.

"Moreover," he went on, giving me a hopeful look, "I am thirsty, and it is too early to go to the Ciào Ciào for a coffee. None of my friends will be there as yet."

"You mean it is too early for the pretty girls to have started their morning parade!" I said tartly, still disturbed by the theory he had propounded at the breakfast table.

He laughed. "Italians are not the only men with an eye for a pretty girl, Melissa! Bird watching, as Leo terms it, is an international, not merely a Mediterranean male habit!"

He slipped off the rail and crossed to the table and lifted up the coffee percolator.

"Come!" he said, "Let me make a fresh pot of coffee, and we can sit together in the sun, and you can finish the breakfast I so rudely interrupted," he glanced at the half eaten roll on the plate in front of which I had been sitting.

"I am not hungry!" I retorted.

"Bene!" he shrugged. "You do not need to eat!" he picked up the piece of roll and flung it into the shrubbery, where a dozen small sparrows pounced greedily on it, "But fresh, strong coffee such as I make will do you good!"

He wiped the crumbs from his fingers, picked up the coffee pot, and departed kitchenwards.

I was put out by his actions. Without being downright rude, how could I tell him to go? He would only be amused if I said that I had work to do, because he knew that the day was my own until late in the afternoon, when I would have to prepare the dinner for the "family."

I was still trying to think of some excuse to get him to leave, when he returned to the table with two cups and the coffee pot, and sat down opposite me.

"Don't you think you are going to find it lonely here all day on your own?" he asked as he waited for me to pour the coffee. "Have you any plans as to how you are going to fill in your time?"

"I thought of going to Alghero, and looking at the shops."

"I shall drive you there," he offered.

"Not till the afternoon!" I continued hastily. "This morning I intended to try to work out a time-table for the work I plan to do with Dirk when I start tutoring him next week."

"That won't take all morning!" he laughed, "so why not let me take you to Alghero this morning and show you around the town. There are a number of interesting corners of the old town I should like to show you."

"I like exploring places on my own!" I wasn't going to let him talk me into anything. "When you are with someone, you can't always stand and stare for as long as you want at the things that appeal to you."

"I would let you stand and stare all day!" he teased me, "if that is what you want to do!"

I gave a sigh of exasperation and said frankly.

"Carlo! You are making it difficult for me to say that I would rather be on my own today, without seeming impolite!"

I shook my head. "I want to be by myself for a little. I want to sunbathe and read or potter about the garden as the mood takes me! After a year of living the regimented life of a girls' boarding school, to do my own thing, when I want to, is a luxury I have been looking forward to!"

Carlo looked from me to the bunch of white marguerites which he had gathered for me the previous afternoon, and which I had arranged in a pottery jar on the table.

"If you had not kept my moon daisies, I might have thought that my company was not to your liking, Melissa, but, yes—" he smiled at me, "I can understand that there are times when one wants to be alone," he drained his cup of coffee and stood up. "So, now, since you wish it, I shall leave you to your own company."

"There is one thing, however," he took a pencil and notebook from his pocket and scribbled a number on it. "Promise me, since Jake and your uncle are out of reach for you today—that if you feel too lonely, or if you feel the need of company, you will telephone me," he handed me a scrap of paper.

I followed him out to his car, waved him goodbye, and returned to the house to wash the breakfast dishes before going outside to sunbathe on the terrace below the patio.

However, in spite of my professed desire to be alone, after twenty minutes of lying in the sun, I grew restless.

I had been sincere when I told Carlo that I wanted to be alone, but I found that despite the Devlins' large and sprawling villa I was not enjoying being on my own.

Being alone is different from loneliness, and it was loneliness I was becoming conscious of, as I lay there in the sun. The villa was remote from the main road. It was even remote from its nearest neighbor, for although the Devlin's large and sprawling villa was less than a quarter of a mile away, it was almost completely hidden from sight by the especially high, barbed wire covered wall which Devlin had erected round it, and the thick hedge of tall, evergreen magnolias which grew on our side of the wall, to hide its bleakness, added to the general impression of complete isolation.

Possibly if Carlo had not advanced his insane theory that morning, that he thought that someone was making a deliberate and determined attempt on my life, I might not have felt so conscious of my loneliness; so conscious of every unexpected noise: so ridiculously certain that as I lay sunbathing in the garden, I was being spied on by someone on the shrub covered hillside on the other side of the cove, for, from time to time as I gazed across the bay to the opposite crescent of land, I had caught the glint of sunlight on glass, as though someone in the car which I could see parked at the top of the track which Jake and I had used that morning, was looking across at me with binoculars.

I tried to tell myself that once again I was letting my over vivid imagination run away with me, but when the telephone bell buzzed unexpectedly I was so tensed with nerves, that I jumped to my feet too quickly, sending the blood rushing to my brain, and causing a momentary feeling of giddiness.

I had to lower my head to my knees, and give myself time to come to, before I went indoors to answer it.

I was taken aback to hear Jake's voice on the line.

"I thought I'd give you a ring, Melissa," he said

cheerfully. "I expect you are feeling a bit dreary, being on your own. How are things going?"

"I was beginning to wish I had taken Carlo up on his offer to take me sightseeing in Alghero this morning," I told him. "I did not realize quite how quiet the villa would seem, after the hustle and bustle of school life, and the company I have enjoyed since I came here!" I sighed. "I just can't settle to anything!"

"So Carlo offered to take you out this morning, did he?" said Jake gruffly. "You watch it where he is concerned, Melissa," he warned me. "He is a nice guy, and we are good friends. We have a lot in common, but that does not include my best girl!" he teased.

"Your girl?" I shook my head at the receiver. "Come off it! You aren't going to tell me that you haven't looked at anyone else in—how many years is it since you last took me out?"

"Touché!" he chuckled. "Who has been giving me away?"

"I have my spies everywhere!" I retorted. "So now, since I am not, in fact, your special girl, can you give me another reason why I should not go out with Carlo?"

Jake did not reply immediately, but after a pause he said. "That is the only one I can think of, Melissa!"

"Well, it isn't a very good one!" I said crisply, and because I wanted to change the subject I added, "Did you have any other reason for phoning me, apart from the fact you wanted to know what I was doing with myself?"

"Yes, as a matter of fact, I did," he replied.

"Leo and I have finished work on our plane much more quickly than we expected, and I was wondering if you would like to come for a flip this afternoon?"

"I should love to!" I agreed readily, "but no aerobatics, please! I remember the times you used to take me up back home, and try to make me sick by looping the loop!"

"And you wouldn't oblige!" he chuckled. "Melissa, it is no wonder you don't think much of me, after all the teasing you had to endure from me in those days!"

"That was a long time ago!" I sighed.

"A long time ago!" he repeated. "But we are wasting time with all these reminiscences. It is almost twelve, and Leo has reserved a table for the three of us at the sea food place, so I shall have to hurry if I have to come and collect you and take you in to Alghero."

I laid the receiver back on its cradle. Listening to Jake's voice, recalling the old days, made me more aware than ever how much he meant to me.

It would be difficult for me to put him out of my life and out of my thoughts, but I would have to. It would not be fair to him, or to Jane, if by some unintentional look, or word or gesture, I betrayed the depths of my feelings for him. I foresaw that the weeks I would have to spend in his company while here in Sardinia, were going to be very difficult, unless I could find something, or someone, to preoccupy my leisure.

Right on cue, almost as if to resolve the problem for me, the telephone rang again. This time the caller was Carlo Roncardi, to ask if he could give me a lift into town in the afternoon. When I told him of my new plans, he gave a mock sigh.

"So you prefer Jake to me after all!"

"Don't be silly!" I said quickly. "A girl can change her mind! If your invitation to note in Alghero holds good for tomorrow, I shall be delighted to accept it!"

Yes, I thought to myself, as I confirmed that I would be ready to leave when Carlo called for me at ten o'clock the following morning, Carlo Roncardi was the answer to my problem.

Jake might not approve of my going out and about with his friend, but what I did was no business of his from now on. He had his Jane. I had my own life to lead.

SIXTEEN

I looked forward to my afternoon with Jake with mixed feelings. It was not perhaps wise of me to have accepted the invitation, but my response had been automatic, as it had been in the old days when he had asked me to fly with him over the glens and mountains of Angus, when we had viewed from the air the herds of deer that roamed there, and followed the hill tracks which we often walked along at weekends.

Today, after leaving Leo at the airport with Bettina, who had joined us for lunch, it was over the wild mountains of Barbagia that we flew, with Jake pointing out to me the very many nuraghic and neolithic ruins that were scattered throughout the island, and explaining to me how from this height, photographs and even the naked eye could detect, from the degrees and types of vegetation, where old townships had been, and where, hidden by centuries of wind blown sand and scree and the cover of an invading wilderness of grass and weeds the remains of the outposts built by the Romans who had once occupied the island, still lay.

It was like old times, being with Jake like this, and listening with interest to his pleasant voice, even if he had to shout to make himself heard as he pointed out the places of interest, that I almost forgot the present and with it the knowledge that a close friendship, such as ours had been, could not continue on the same terms after marriage.

I was brought back abruptly to this reality when Jake flew low to point out another area of ruins, where little dolls, who were real people, were moving around. One of them looked up at the aircraft and waved.

"That is Jane," he laughed. "She always waves. She says it is a flashback to her childhood, when she used to wave to the train drivers at the level crossing near her home!"

He circled the site a couple of times, flying down low enough for me to distinguish each member of the team, before banking to fly back down a valley, between hills of sheep and goats, over orchards and vineyards until we came to the coast, where he went out over the sea, then came round again to fly over the promontory on which the Villas Gelsomino and Magnolia were built.

Here we could see figures in the Devlins' swimming pool, and again Jake flew low enough, but not dangerously so, so that we could make out individuals—Dirk, who scrambled from the water to wave to us, Sally, lying on a deck chair on the patio, and Eve seated at a table, typing.

"Enjoy the flip?" asked Jake as he swung me down from the plane a few minutes later, holding me by the waist, and smiling at me.

I smiled back, but I had to make an effort to keep my smile from wavering, because the touch of Jake's arms, the gentle pressure of his fingers round my waist as he continued to hold me, stirred up anew that tingling, electric emotion of my awareness to him, which I was trying so hard to overcome.

"Of course I did!" I assured him, pushing his hands away, "and I liked the geography lesson that went with it!" I moved away from him to walk across the patch of field to the spot where Leo and Bettina were waiting for us.

Why, oh why, I thought bitterly, had there to be a Jane. Why, oh why couldn't Jake react to the same chemistry which set my heart beating unsteadily at his touch!

"Bully for you, Melissa!" Bettina greeted me with a grin. "I wouldn't go up in one of these toy planes for the world! Weren't you scared?"

"I don't scare easily," I forced a smile. "In any case, I have flown with Jake before, and at least this time he didn't try to throw the plane all over the sky, as he did the last time!"

"There was no point!" grinned Jake, joining us. "I have tried all the tricks I know to impress you!"

Bettina winked at me. "He wants you to tell him what a wonderful pilot he is," she whispered. "Men are all the same! If you want to have them eat out of your hands, you have to flatter them, and make them feel wonderful, even if they aren't!"

"Jake wouldn't believe me if I told him he was wonderful!" I said scornfully. "We know each other too well!"

Bettina shrugged. "Every male likes to be flattered, even if he is only the boy next door!"

"Come along, Bettina," Leo gave her a nudge. "If there is any flattery going, save it to tell me how much you enjoyed my driving this afternoon!"

Bettina made an expressive face. "Enjoy your driving?" she stressed the word "enjoy." "My dear Leo, the next time we go out in a car, I am going to be the one behind the wheel! These island roads are not the race track at Monza, as you seem to think!"

They bickered happily in the back seat of the car on the return journey to Alghero, where we stopped to collect the record I had ordered, before returning to the villa.

"I shall be working tomorrow, Bettina," Leo reminded the girl as we dropped her off at the entrance to the Devlin place, "but don't forget about the barbecue on Wednesday!"

"Yes, I am sorry we shall be working, and that you will be on your own all day tomorrow," Jake reversed the car back to the gateway of the Villa Gelsomino.

"Not to worry!" I said brightly, "Carlo is taking me out for the day, to show me places of interest in Alghero. There is some church he particularly wants to show me, one associated with the fishing community."

"That will be the Chapel of the Madonna di Remedio," said Jake with a scowl. "I wanted to take you there myself, because I knew it was the kind of place that would appeal to you. It is full of atmosphere—old and dark and somehow homely. The votive lamps are like miniature ships, and the Madonna herself is surrounded by coral, as a reminder that coral fishing plays, and always has played, an important part in the life of Alghero."

He turned to me, "Don't laugh at me, Melissa, but truth to tell, the first time I saw it, I thought of you and how much you would like it, honey."

Honey. That was his nickname for me, from the days when I had looked up the meaning of my Christian name in a book, and discovered that Melissa meant honey. In fact, he had only reverted to calling me Melissa after he went to college, and started taking out his succession of pretty girls.

Now, when he called me by the pet name again, it didn't please me. It was almost as if he was mocking me, seeing me still as a romantic teenager with a love of old houses and old ruins, and a voracious reader of romantic, Gothic novels, and so I said crisply.

"Carlo told me he was sure it was a place that I would find intriguing. He is going to find out more about it for me, so that he can tell me its history when he sees me tomorrow."

I stepped from the car, and Jake followed me, slamming the door so noisily that Leo looked at him in suprprise, and I realized that he was in a pet because Carlo, and not he, was going to show me the Chapel!

My lips tightened in anger. There was no need for Jake to create a scene because I was going out with his friend. I was free to go with whom I pleased, where I pleased.

In any case, if Jake had been under the impression that Carlo Roncardi had invited me out to flirt with me, he was quite wrong. We spent a very pleasant time together exploring the old town, while he told me of its past history, dating back to the days of the Dorias, and of its Catallan connections.

We went to his sister Magdalena's house for lunch, and she gave me several Sardinian recipes, including one which Carlo said was a favorite of Jake's, and which, as a sop to his hurt feelings, I prepared for dinner that night.

With a somewhat shame-faced grimace, he admitted that I had spent the day usefully, and the others were so pleased with my cooking that they told me they would leave me in charge of the preparations for the barbecue the following evening.

SEVENTEEN

The barbecue on Wednesday was to celebrate Max's birthday, and everyone was looking forward to it.

Although it was dusk before we reached the picnic spot, the air was still warm, and after we had set out the tables and all the other paraphernalia associated with such an occasion on the beach, and the men had started a fire of wood and twigs under the spit where Jake had undertaken to roast the two small suckling pigs which Magdalena had brought, Bettina suggested that there would be time for a quick swim before the food was ready.

Bettina and I went to change into our bathing suits in the Rover, and Carlo lit another fire so that we could warm ourselves at it when we came out of the water, and disappeared into the gloom of the nearby hills to collect a further supply of twigs and branches for the fuel store, while Dirk and Magdalena's children collected driftwood which had been washed up on the shore by the waves.

In the far horizon, to the west, there were still a few reddish streaks from the afterglow of the setting sun, but nightfall soon took over and only the red glow of the fires' blaze, and the paler glow of the rising moon, lit up the party on the beach.

Bettina and Dirk were the only ones from the Villa Magnolia who came into the water. Sally was not keen, in case she caught a chill, and Eve did not want to spoil her new and expensive hair-do by pushing it tightly under a bathing cap. I could understand how she felt, for although I did not like her new hair style, which was very fussy and curly, I could see that she was very proud of it, possibly because she thought it made her look less what she termed "old-maidish" than the smooth, sleek Spanish style she had worn when I had first seen her.

There was a lot of shouting and screaming as Mike and Stan chased the girls they had met on their weekend holiday, into the water and tried to duck them under. Dirk looked somewhat apprehensive at their fun and games, so I suggested that he should join Magdalena's family, who, as usual were kicking a ball about the sands, while Bettina and I swam out to twin rocks which stood out, like small islands, about twenty yards from the shore where we were picnicking, although they were not too far from the cliffs which curved round the bay.

It was a curious sensation, swimming in the ink dark waters. Alongside me, in her black costume, only Bettina's limbs and face showed, with an eerie, ghostly pallor, as she moved along, and my own white costume seemed to take on a strange phosphorescent glow.

We clambered up on to adjacent rocks, and

stood, silhouetted against the night sky, looking back at the merry party on the beach. It was difficult to make out who was who among the moving, shadowy figures, for even the children had elongated forms against the sparking, blazing glow of the fires.

Only Jake's face, redly reflecting the flames as he turned the spit, was plainly visible, and as if he sensed that we were looking in his direction, he waved to us.

There was a triumphant cry of "Goal" from Max, followed by a shout of "Foul! Foul!" from Tomaso.

"Aren't they enjoying themselves!" Bettina called across to me. "You would think that Max was fifteen instead of forty-six today!"

A cloud crossed the face of the moon, and the silver glow on the rocks on which we stood, and on the water of the bay, turned to blackness. I shivered with a sudden sensation of uneasiness.

"Bettina, let's get back to the shore!" I called to her, and lowered myself into the dark water.

As I did so, something caught at my ankles and pulled me downwards to the sea bed with a violent tug. Seconds before the water closed over my head, I managed to utter a shrill scream, but quickly closed my mouth again as the salt water poured into it.

I kicked and kicked to free myself from the tentacles which clung to me, pressing into my ankles like vicious fingers. For one moment I managed to kick myself free and went shooting to the surface, calling for help, but the groping tentacles gripped my ankles once again, and I was pulled down, down, until I thought my lungs would burst with my need to breathe.

I gave a final weak kick, and miraculously whatever had tangled round my legs slithered away, and I rose to the surface again, and came up, spluttering for air, alongside Bettina.

"Melissa! I heard you scream and came back for you! Is it cramp?" she looked at me anxiously in the light of the moon which had re-appeared from behind the cloud.

"I got tangled up in some sea-weed or something!" I gasped the word painfully. "I'm afraid I panicked a bit, because I thought it was pulling me down deliberately! It was horrible!"

My swimming strokes were as weak and wavery as my voice, and I was going to ask Bettina to help me to the shore, when I felt another hand touch my shoulder, and Jake's voice said comfortingly,

"Lie on your back, honey. I'll take you to the beach!"

"What happened?" Max and Tomaso came rushing up to us as Jake lifted me from the water. "Did you take cramp?"

I shook my head, as Jake put me down on my feet. "No, I got tangled in some weed or other as I slipped from the rock."

I shivered again, and again Jake lifted me in his arms and this time he carried me across to the bonfire which Carlo had lit, before setting me down on the ground, and patting my chilled hands to bring the warmth back to them.

Jane came hurrying toward us, with my towel, and briskly rubbed at my arms and legs saying,

"You ought to get out of your damp suit at once, Melissa. You are shivering with cold!"

"I shall be all right in a minute," I replied, taking the towel from her, and vigorously rubbing my shoulders. "It was just that for the moment, I got such a fright! I thought I would never be able to pull myself free!"

"You would have been all right," said Jake harshly. "I heard you call the first time you went down, and I knew where to swim to—"

"You should have seen him!" said Sally. "He shot into the water as if he was jet propelled. He had almost reached the rock when you yelled again!"

A smell of very burnt pig drifted toward us and drew everyone's attention to the improvised roasting spit. Leo darted away to rescue our supper, driving the children ahead of him to give him a hand, while Eve came running across from the car, with my clothes, and arranged a windbreak so that I could change in privacy beside the fire.

I was about to whip off my damp costume when Carlo Roncardi appeared from the hillside behind us, and came striding to the fire with a bundle of wood to fling on the blaze.

Magdalena rushed up to her brother to explain what had happened, and to drag him away to let me get dressed in privacy.

In spite of the leaping flames, I still felt chilled after I had dressed myself, and my teeth chattered together as I held my hands out to the blaze.

Bettina and the others had also dressed themselves to be ready for the feast, for the rising night breeze did not encourage anyone to sit around in damp suits, and they too came to warm themselves by the fire. Jake noticed I was still shivering, and gallantly whipped off his woollen polo-necked sweater which, in spite of my protests, he pulled down over my head and shoulders, to give me extra warmth.

It felt so snug and cosy, stretching as it did almost to my knees, that I gave him a very grateful smile as I hugged it around me, and he smiled back at me, giving my waist an affectionate squeeze as he said.

"That's more like my girl! It isn't like you, Melissa, to look so sorry for yourself as you were doing a minute ago!"

"Do you feel like a bite to eat now?" asked Jane, who was handing around the plates of food which Tomaso and Magdalena were doling out.

"I think you would prefer a hot coffee first, Melissa," Carlo came forward and handed me a mug of steaming liquid around which I cupped my hands.

He looked at me with a frown as he added, "Tell me, what exactly happened when you were out at the rock? Magdalena says that you got tangled in some weed which dragged you down, is that the case?"

I nodded. "Look, you can still see the marks on my ankles, where it tangled around them!" I pointed to the peculiar weals which showed red in the firelight.

Jake gave an angry gasp. "I didn't notice them before. But what kind of weed would leave impressions like finger prints?" he asked Carlo.

"Maybe it was an octopus!" squealed Dirk excitedly. "A giant octopus!"

"Around here, my lad, it is men who capture octopuses, not the other way around," Max ruffled the boy's hair.

Carlo dropped to his knees to examine my ankles, and when he stood up again he remarked thoughtfully.

"Yes, these marks could have been made by suckers. But don't worry about them, Melissa," his mouth smiled, but his eyes had a puzzled look in them. "They will have disappeared by morning."

With all the excitement over my adventure, we had almost forgotten Max's birthday, but now Leo and Bettina produced bottles of champagne, and with the popping of corks, the handshakes and the kisses and the presents that everyone had brought for the popular "Professor," to say nothing of the platefuls of delicious food which followed, my moment of misfortune was soon forgotten by everyone else, although once or twice, in the ensuing days, when I went swimming with Jake in the cove before breakfast, a fish brushing my ankle or a piece of weed floating beside me, would bring the incident back to my mind.

EIGHTEEN

The Thursday before I was due to take up my post as Dirk's tutor was the 6th of July, the day of the Fiesta San Antine, when people from all over Sardinia, many of them dressed in their local costumes travel to the little town of Sedillo, near the center of the island, to rejoice in the anniversary of the defeat of the heathens by the Christians.

Jane was very keen to attend the festival, since she felt that since she was staying on the island she should learn as much as possible of its history and culture, but oddly, Carlo, who up till now had devoted a lot of his time taking me to see places of interest, was not at all keen that we should go.

For once, Jake and Carlo were in agreement, but Max and Jane over-rode them, pointing out that it would be a shame to miss seeing one of the most spectacular of the island's festivals, since they might never have the opportunity again.

As usual, the girls next door were asked to join us, but Sally, who had not been feeling well for several days said that she did not feel up to the long and tortuous drive, and she did not want to be over-tired before the arrival of her husband, who was due back from the States in a couple of days.

Eve had a lot of work to do in preparation for

Devlin's arrival, for there was always plenty of mail for her to attend to, and there were also the arrangements for the home-coming party to see to, so she too declined the invitation, leaving Bettina as the sole representative from the Villa Magnolia.

Stan and Mike were taking their two girl friends in the car they had hired, and Jake took Leo, Jane and Max, and would have taken me as well in his Fiat, but Carlo insisted that I should go with him in his Alfa, an arrangement which pleased Bettina as much as it did me, because it meant she could sit beside Leo in the back seat of the Fiat.

Carlo, who knew the twisting mountain roads, led the convoy out of Alghero, through the foothills with their orchards and vineyards and compounds of small palm leaf houses and olive groves. He drove fast, but well, pointing out landmarks as we drove along, telling me of the different costumes worn by the men and women of the villages we passed through, saying that they wore plain ones for every day, and more ornate ones on Sundays and feast days.

As we drove through the narrow streets of the hill town of Ittiri, he slowed down so that I could get a good look at the women in their local dress, and he chaffed me by telling me that I should return to the village on the 25th of July for the procession of Santa Lucia, for that was the day when young girls dress up in their best costumes to go to church and pray to the saint for a husband.

"Marriage is not the be all and end all of a girl's life nowadays!" I spoke sharply.

"A good marriage makes for a good society, Melissa, cara," he said, eyeing me in the driving

180

mirror, "and you are the marrying kind—I don't mean a matriarch—" he grinned, "but someone it would be pleasant to come home to, pleasant to grow old with. No, cara," his voice was strangely serious, "don't put your career first; say 'Yes' to marriage, while you are young!"

I looked away from him, over the poppy sprinkled verges of the road to the vine-clad slopes beyond, and said slowly.

"The 'Yes' would have to be to the right man, Carlo, and," I added with a forced lightness as I turned to look at him, "if this is your way of proposing to me, I am afraid," I shook my head, "the answer is no!"

Carlo's eyes flashed with amusement, then grew serious again. He opened his mouth to speak, then changed his mind and snapped it shut.

For a long time he stared straight ahead, concentrating on his driving, almost as if he was afraid that if he did speak, he might say something he would regret, and it was not until we slowed down once more as we were passing through Thiesi, to join the main highway, which had been built on the site of the first Roman military road on the island, that he said, with a sad shake of his head.

"Cara Melissa! How can such a pretty girl, such an intelligent girl as you are, also be, forgive me, such a stupid girl? You know, surely, that—"

"That you were not really proposing to me!" I interrupted him with a laugh. "Of course, Carlo! I was only teasing when I said that! I know that you like me, and that we enjoy each other's company, but that is all there is to it, for both of us, isn't it?"

181

Even as I was speaking, I found myself thinking that if there hadn't been a Jake, however, it would be easy to fall for this man by my side; very easy. Instinctively I felt myself grow tense, as if these very thoughts were a betrayal of the feeling I had for Jake.

Carlo, who had stopped the car to make sure that the others had taken the correct turning in the village, was not looking at me, but back along the way we had come as he said.

"Yes, my dear. You and I could be no more than very good friends!" He sounded almost regretful.

After a time we reached Macomer, where we joined the procession of vehicles, coming into the town from every direction, to converge on Sedillo, where that evening at seven o'clock, a repetition of the battle which had taken place between heathen and Christian there so many centuries ago, would be re-enacted.

We parked the cars amid the host of other cars in a field near the site of the old battlefield, and joined the throng of people who were making their way on foot, through the archway of St. Constantine, and along a path which led up to a church on a hill. All along the way there were stalls selling souvenirs, ice-cream, candy floss and sweets. There were stalls behind which young pigs were being roasted on spits. There were stalls of balloons and dolls, and all around was to be heard the incessant babble of a dozen different dialects, the sound of tired children wailing, of excited children shouting, and loud speakers thundering out directions. People shoved and pushed and elbowed their way to get to the best vantage point to watch the horse-back battle, which would take place round and round the little church.

In the crush, Max and Jane had disappeared from view, but Jake and Carlo had both taken me by the arm, and were propelling me in the wake of Leo and Bettina and the younger members of our party.

I could scarcely get the opportunity to admire some of the lovely local costumes in the crush, and there were faces in the crowd, lean, dark, intense-looking and cruel-mouthed, which reminded me that we were near the center of the bandit country, and instinctively I clung more tightly to the arms of my companions. This was certainly no place for any young woman to get separated from her friends, yet it would be all too easy to get swept away by the milling, excited crowds which swelled around us.

Carlo edged me into a space in front of the crowd near the church, beside a tumbledown, low wall, and slipped an arm around my waist, as a villainous-looking man, wearing a white head-dress, a red jacket embroidered with gold, a pleated black shirt and black trousers, came rushing along, firing a gun.

This was the signal for the battle to commence. More guns were fired, pale wisps of smoke rose into the deepening blue of the evening sky, horses came charging down from two hills opposite the church, their riders yelling and brandishing sticks, ready for the forthcoming clash. The church bells were ringing with a continuous, monotonous clang; fresh volleys of shot sounded deafeningly close; dust kicked up by the galloping horses filled the air as they thundered past, and from the chaotic fighting, I thought it inevitable that some horses and riders would be injured.

There were screams and cheers from the crowds as the fighting horsemen challenged each other over and over again, and as the battle grew fiercer, the spectators grew more and more excited and pressed forward, closer and closer to the track, pushing and shoving without a care for whoever stood in their way. Carlo's arm slipped from my waist, and he was forced away from me. I clung more tightly than ever to Jake, and he to me, for I was convinced that any moment, if the crowd got out of control, I would be pushed into the path of the madly charging horses, whose foaming mouths and heavy breathing made them look like fearsome creatures from another world.

I screamed to Jake above the din.

"Let's get away from here!"

He nodded, and we turned around, away from the spectacle to climb over the low, crumbling wall behind us, which was now more of a hazard than a protection. I stood for a moment, above the crowd, while Jake put up his arms to help me down from the pile of stones. At that very minute another, single shot rang out, and I was almost whirled off my feet as something punched forcibly into the camera case slung over my shoulder, and pinged off the buckle with a metallic echo.

Beside me a woman screamed and shouted that she had been shot, but only those nearest to her heard her scream or saw the blood on the back of her hand, where it had been grazed by the bullet ricocheting off my sturdy case.

Jake grabbed at me. "For heaven's sake, Melissa, get away from here!" With no thought for those who came in his way, he dragged me after him through the crowds, and Carlo, who had been only a few paces away from us on the other side of the wall, fought his way to us, and together we managed to push a passage through the mob, to regain the comparative quiet of the path which led back through the archway.

I was trembling, and Jake was as white as a sheet as we hurried along. Carlo, who had been close enough to us to hear the woman scream and also to see me whirl round on the wall, asked to have a look at my camera case, and studied it with a grim expression.

"This confirms what I told you already—if I needed further confirmation," he added, tight-lipped. "Too many accidents are happening to you for them all to be coincidences, including your near drowning at the beach the other night," he told me. "Then I could have sworn that fingers, not tentacles had caused the marks on your ankles, but I did not want to make a public pronouncement at the time."

I gaped at him. "What do you mean?"

"Melissa," he frowned. "I have no doubts at all now, that someone is trying to kill you!"

"But why?" I cried, looking at Carlo with disbelief.

"That is what we must find out," he said gravely. "That is why we have been keeping you under observation these past days."

"Me? Under observation?" I stared at him blankly.

"Yes, Melissa," said Jake. "That is why Carlo has been hanging around you so much! He is a policeman, on duty!"

"I was sent from the mainland regarding a series of blackmail cases here," Carlo explained. "It was thought that my local knowledge might be of help."

We had reached the car park, and Carlo opened the door of his Alfa and helped me inside, while Jake crawled into the narrow ledge of a seat behind us.

"After the string of strange incidents in which you were involved," he went on, "and particularly when we learned that no blond and bearded sailor answering to the description you had given us was a crew member of either of the warships, we realized you had been deliberately lured away from the dance because you were you, and not any young girl, and since the case I am involved in is concerned with very wealthy people, and since you had worked in a school attended by the daughters of the very wealthy, I wondered if there could be some connection?"

Carlo's eyes probed into mine. "So now, tell me Melissa," he asked. "When did you start having these accidents? Did anything similar occur before you came to Sardinia?" Carlo's fingers pressed on my wrists as if he wanted to shake a helpful answer from me.

"I still don't understand!" I gasped. What was happening could not be happening to me! "Life was quite normal before I came here! There were no accidents. No near accidents. No unpleasantness. Nothing!"

Carlo continued to stare at me.

"Then what have you seen, or heard, since you came here, which has made you the fly in someone's ointment?"

I shook my head in protest. "Nothing!" I glared at him. "It is sheer coincidence that all those things happened either to, or near me! Sheer coincidence!" I insisted.

"No," said Carlo firmly. "These incidents were planned to look like accidents. They were well planned, too, because they appeared so—so natural in a way! But there have been too many of them. They roused my suspicion, and now I have proof that you were the target for them all, so please, Melissa," he pleaded, "for your own life's sake, think back to the days, the hours, before the first one occurred. What did you see, on the day of your arrival? Did you perhaps even overhear a snatch of conversation on the plane?" he hazarded a guess.

I shook my head. "These things don't make sense!" I cried. "I have seen nothing, heard nothing, that others around me could not have seen or heard, so why pick on me?"

"Perhaps the man who broke into your room the first night thought you would be able to recognize him again!" Jake hazarded a guess, as he put his hand on my shoulder to give it a comforting squeeze. "Perhaps if the police let it be known that you could not do so, he will leave you alone, rather than stick out his neck further!" he glanced at Carlo, all the while stroking my neck to relieve the tension of my muscles, and his fingers were so

187

gentle and almost caressing in their action that I closed my eyes, and tried to put from me the fears Carlo had conjured up, and surrendered to the thrill of his touch.

NINETEEN

Jake returned to his own car to sit there until the mock battle was over and Max and the others returned to join him, but Carlo drove me back to Alghero with all speed, since he wished to contact his brother-in-law as soon as possible, about the latest attempt on my life to discuss what further steps could be taken for my protection.

With so many holiday makers in the area, a spate of thefts in the hotels, sheep-stealing in the interior, to say nothing of the continued violence of family vendettas, Captain Patrizio Venerdi's resources were stretched to their limits, and after a lot of discussion, it was reluctantly decided that it would have to be mainly up to myself to keep out of trouble.

I was warned not to go off on my own anywhere, and to keep a sharp look out at all times for anything or anyone that looked suspicious. Carlo himself would, whenever possible, keep an eye on me, as he had been doing, and the others in the villa would also be told to be on their guard.

When we talked over the position in the villa that evening, Jake was keen for me to join the party at the site, so that I would not be left alone in the house for so much of the day, but Carlo pointed out that the site was an isolated one, and it would be easier for the police to deal with anything which arose if I stayed where I was.

In any event, everyone agreed I would be perfectly safe in the mornings once I started tutoring Dirk, because the Villa Magnolia was so well guarded, although it was also agreed that nothing would be said to the members of the Devlin household about what was going on, in case it upset the girls, and particularly Sally, whom Jane said was a few weeks pregnant.

The following morning, Jake was very loath to leave me alone in the house, but he had undertaken to do some aerial photography for the site engineer of a proposed new marina near Olbia, and it was such a good contract he did not want to opt out.

I convinced him that I was not at all worried about being on my own, and pointed out that it would be most difficult for anyone to approach the villa during the hours of daylight without being seen. I would be keeping a watchful eye for intruders, and at the first sign of anything untoward, I would do as I had been told, and telephone the police station immediately.

In any event, Carlo had promised to come to visit me in the afternoon, and stay with me until Jake or one of the others returned, so there was nothing for him to worry about, although I was touched by his concern for me.

He stayed with me as long as he could after the others left, and it was only when Leo tapped his watch significantly that they, too, reluctantly left the villa.

I waved them goodbye, and once they were out

of sight, I went around the house, shutting and bolting every shutter, and making sure that all doors leading into the house were locked, before I set about my household duties. However, my courage slowly ebbed with each unexpected sound that broke the silence of the lonely house, and finally I retired to the study, locked myself in, and sat down at the desk, with the telephone only inches from my hand.

I attempted to write letters to my family and friends to fill in time, but my first letter got no further than the date—the seventh of July—for as I wrote it down, the date struck a chord in my memory, and somehow or other, I associated it with a color—coral—pink—yes, that was it, pink, but why should this particular date ring a bell? It was no one's birthday. It meant nothing to me. And why did pink suggest itself at the same time?

I doodled the date, with roses, and wrote pink several times, in the hope that this would jog my memory, and after the date and the color I scrawled a number of question marks which increased in size to the end of the line, and I was so preoccupied with my puzzle that I forgot about my loneliness for a time.

Finally, however, with the riddle still unsolved, I pushed the page aside and steeled myself to go to the kitchen and make some sandwiches and coffee for my mid-day meal, which I sat and ate in the study, still irritated with myself for not solving the problem of the pink seventh!

Carlo arrived, as arranged, on the stroke of two, and I was so pleased to see him, I could have hugged him. I made fresh coffee for him, and we went out to the patio to drink it, for I felt in need of some fresh air after spending the morning indoors.

"How would you like to go for a car run, Melissa?" he suggested. "I expect you are pretty fed up with sitting about the house. Or, what would be even more of a change, I could take you to the Grotto of Neptune by sea!"

"The Grotto of Neptune?" I frowned as an elusive memory surfaced and vanished again.

He nodded. "It is one of Alghero's beauty spots which I haven't had time to show you as yet."

I looked at him doubtfully, and he smiled and said,

"You will be quite all right there, Melissa. I shall see to that, but," he looked at the fine cotton blouse I was wearing, "since we are traveling by sea, I would advise you to take a warm cardigan or blazer. The salt breeze can be quite chilly."

I was delighted at the prospect of getting away from the house, and hurried upstairs to get a jacket. I had reached the landing when the telephone rang, and I paused wondering if Carlo would answer it for me.

I heard him lift the receiver and say "Pronto" and waited for him to call me, but the call was obviously for him for he did not summon me, and I could hear the murmur of his voice as he replied, although I could not distinguish what he was saying.

I went into my room, tidied my hair and freshened up my make-up, before taking a long woollen cardigan from the wardrobe, and, slinging it around my shoulders, I made my way back downstairs.

Carlo was waiting for me in the hall, and there was a frown on his handsome face.

"Melissa, I am sorry, but I am afraid we shall have to postpone our trip. The call was from a colleague, who is at the hospital where they have taken a man who may be able to help me in my inquiries about the blackmail case. He had been shot," he added, tight-lipped.

"Then obviously you must go to the hospital!" I told him.

"Yes," he bit his lip, "but I cannot take you there with me. I may be gone for an hour, perhaps two. I am sorry, Melissa. You will just have to stay here on your own until I get back!"

I sighed, and said hopefully, "Perhaps you won't be too long! I shall keep my fingers crossed!"

I shrugged the cardigan from my shoulders and dropped it carelessly on a nearby chair, as I followed him to the front door to wave him a dejected farewell.

Almost before his car was out of sight, the telephone rang again.

"Sally here," said a voice which was so indistinct I had to strain my ears to hear what was being said. 'Is that you Melissa?"

"I can hardly hear you!" I raised my voice. "It's a bad line! Is that you, Sally?"

"Yes!" the faint voice confirmed. "Listen, I am sorry to trouble you, but I wonder if you could help me out?"

"Yes? What is it?"

"As you know, this is the afternoon we all flock to Francesco's salon," she hesitated. "Eve and Bettina have already left, and I was waiting for Pino to arrive, to keep an eye on Dirk, as he usually does on Fridays, but he hasn't turned up yet, and I can't hang on any longer or I shall miss my appointment, and Richard comes home tomorrow!" the wail of her voice came and went on waves of weak sound.

"So you want me to come and baby-sit, is that it?" I shouted into the telephone, hoping that she would hear me more plainly than I could hear her.

"Could you?" she squeaked. "Right away?"

"Right away!" I agreed cheerfully, delighted at the prospect of not spending another minute alone in the Villa Gelsomino.

"You dear girl!" I detected a note of relief in the whispering voice before she replaced the receiver, but she could not have felt as relieved as I did!

After putting the receiver on the cradle, I scribbled a brief message under my doodles on the writing pad, and stuck it against the telephone, where Jake, or whoever arrived home first, would be bound to see it, should I myself not be back before them.

"I have gone next door to baby-sit—Melissa."

I picked up my cardigan and handbag, and left the house, securely locking the door behind me, and prudently glancing up and down the road to make sure that no one was loitering about in wait for me, I went hurrying along to the Villa Magnolia.

To my surprise, the front gate leading into the Devlins' garden was open, and there was no sign either of the gate-keeper or his guard dogs. I hurried up the driveway, and under the second arched wall, to reach the front door.

I rang the bell, but no one answered, although, like the gate the front door stood ajar, and from inside the house I could hear music from a transistor.

Tentatively I stepped into the hall and called. "I'm here, Sally!"

There was a movement behind me, and as I half turned, something caught me a sickening blow on the side of the head, and I slithered to the ground.

When I came to, I was lying on the floor of a small estate car, tied hand and foot, with strips of plastic across my mouth. Beside me, but stretched along the seat, I could see Dirk, his face pale, his breathing heavy, his eyes closed. He was not bound as I was, but I guessed he had been drugged.

I tried to struggle up to a sitting position, but I was secured in some way to the floor, and all I could see of the driver, the only other occupant of the car, was the sheen of yellow hair curling over his shoulder, and with a growing sense of fear, I deduced that this could be the fair-haired sailor who had attacked me outside the Mermaid Cave!

The car stopped under a canopied roof, and the driver deftly flung a rug over me and the boy, before getting out of the vehicle. I wondered where we had been taken, and why, and what was going to happen to us. My head still ached from the blow which had rendered me unconscious at

Dirk's house, and I could not form coherent thoughts. My arms and legs, and indeed the whole of my body was sore from bruising, caused no doubt, when I had been manhandled into the car, and I could scarcely breathe because of the rug over my nostrils.

The car started up again, and from the speed at which we were going, it would seem the driver was in a great hurry, I judged that we were out of the town now, for I could detect little sound of other traffic, and then, after a time, I was made achingly aware that we had left the main road and were bumping along some dirt track, or even across a rough field.

I wanted to scream out in agony each time I was jolted, and pain shot through my body, but the tape across my lips prevented me. Then, to my relief, the car slowed to a halt. The driver got out, slamming his door behind him. The door to the rear of the vehicle was opened. The blanket which covered me was dragged off. I looked up, blinking, and found myself staring into a face which was framed in a tangle of fair hair, but it was no stranger I was looking at! The dark, angry eyes that blazed a look of hate at me as I lay there, helpless, were the eyes of Eve Yuille!

My utter astonishment must have shown in my face, because she laughed joylessly as she bent over me and undid the ropes which tied me to the seat belt anchors on the floor, and dragging me out onto the rough grass of a field which stretched out across a desolate foreland, and sloped to the steep cliffs on the left, she snarled.

"This time, young woman, your luck has run

out! This time you will not survive to give us away!"

Spurning me with her foot, she returned to the car, lifted the still unconscious Dirk from the seat, and dumped him down beside me. He moaned faintly, and I glared up at her, wondering what she was up to, wondering how on earth I had become involved in her scheme, and what was going to happen to Dirk and me.

"Yes, Melissa Gilchrist," she went on, "I am the one who arranged for the attempts on your life, who tried to drown you! It was an unlucky day for you when you crossed my path!"

She glanced at her watch, then in the direction of the cliffs, and I guessed that she was waiting for someone, and growing impatient at being kept waiting.

"But of course, you have no idea what I am talking about, have you?" she was speaking nervously now, "and yet you could have spoiled it all for me! You could have given me away, after all my weeks of careful planning, after all the arrangements had been finalized! Yes!" she glared at me. "You could have spoiled everything!" she repeated. "You could have balked me of my revenge, and I was not going to have that! No innocent-eyed little blonde was going to get in my way! You were expendable!"

I gulped and choked on the saliva which trickled down my throat, and Eve laughed, enjoying my discomfiture as she talked on.

"You see," her eyes glinted angrily, "I was in love, passionately in love with Richard Devlin, even before the death of his first wife. After she died, I was certain that I could make him love me too! Yes," she said bitterly. "I loved Richard Devlin—once. I did everything for him! I pushed him to where he is today! I encouraged him! I kept an eye on his business, his brat! I was the woman in his life! The one he turned to when he needed comfort, and I was certain that in spite of Bettina's efforts, for she wanted him too—that in the end, he would realize he could not do without me. He would marry me!"

She clenched her hands together in such fury of rage, that the skin of her knuckles went white.

"Yes, he would have married me too, if he hadn't met Sally, and fallen unreasoningly in love with her, and married her, and I meant nothing to him any more. Nothing!" her voice grew vicious. "I was only his faithful secretary, someone to order around, someone for his new wife to order around, a well oiled cog in his household, that was all! So," her gaze fell on Dirk, "I determined to make him pay for what he had done to me. I determined to hurt him as he had hurt me, and I knew the way to do it!

"He worships his son. He would do anything for him. If anything were to happen to Dirk, he would be a broken man—"

I looked at her with loathing, but she scarcely seemed to be aware of my presence as she rambled on.

"I have a brother, who lives on his charm—a confidence man, in fact. Because of his odd profession, he knows a number of odd people, and one of the odd people who live on the twilight world of crime was a man I knew. A blackmailer, although I hadn't guessed this, and a man I could make use of, because of this!"

She glanced again at her watch, and frowned impatiently as she continued. "Francesco hears a lot of gossip from his ladies, you see! They let their hair down in more ways than one when they visit him in his salon, and he checks their information later, and then uses it to his advantage!

"In this instance, however, I am the blackmailer, who used the threat of exposure to get him to do what I wanted! He was the man who tried to kill you, as he is the man who will provide me with an unbreakable alibi for this afternoon!"

Unexpectedly she whipped off her blonde wig and revealed a head of hair which had been cut short, like soft feathers around her neat head. It was a style completely different from the one she had worn the previous day, and one which must have taken hours to create.

"Clever, isn't it?" she gave a pleased laugh. "Francesco cut my hair like this last week, but I covered it with that fussy black wig, so that today, when I appear from his cubicle, like this, everyone will think it has been newly done! People will even have heard him talk to me in his little private room! So how could anyone suspect that I had anything to do with Dirk's kidnapping? After all," she sneered down at Dirk, "everyone knows how much I dote on the brat! But oh!" she gloated, "How I am looking forward to seeing Richard suffer tomorrow, when he arrives home and finds out what has happened! He will turn on Sally for not looking after Dirk! He will turn on Bettina! He will even turn on me!" she sniggered. "But he will pay the ransom we demand, and then—"

She stopped speaking at the sound of footsteps crunching on the dry ground, and turned round, and I looked in the same direction, and now I understood why I was here. Why I had been a threat to Eve. The man coming toward us was the man who had ogled me at Milan airport! As I looked at him, the scene came clearly into my memory, and I remembered the words spoken to him by the unseen woman, who must have been Eve.

"Danny! Can't you keep your mind off pretty girls for a second while we talk business?"

I remembered, too, the man's reply, and the rest of the curious conversation, and Eve, when she had been introduced to me a few hours later at Alghero airport had immediately recognized me, and although she realized I had not seen her in Milan, she appreciated that I must have heard all that had been said at the airport, when the date, the time, the place, even the fact that she was taking a boy with her to the rendezvous had been discussed in my presence. Most damning of all, she had mentioned her brother Danny by name, and she would be traced through that alone!

Yes, once the kidnap became a reality, if I recalled the incident, all would be up with them, and Eve wasn't prepared to take this chance. On the other hand, she was determined on her revenge, and the answer was simple. I had to be got out of the way, permanently, before the kidnap took place!

"Where does she fit in?" the man looked down

at me. "Don't you remember the girl at the airport?" Eve asked.

"Ah!" he nodded. "So you want them both overboard now, is that it?" he asked dispassionately. "It is not going to be easy," he shook his head. "You will have to help get the girl to the Grotto, Eve."

"I can't!" she snapped. "I haven't the time, and it is your fault! You were late! And I told you time was of the essence! I have to get back so that Francesco can keep his next appointment!"

"At least you can drag her to the top of the cliff path!" he snapped. "I could haul them both down from there!" he stooped to lift Dirk up, but as Eve bent toward me, I rolled away from her.

She grabbed at me again, but although my feet were tied together, I bent my knees and lashed out at her. She screeched in anger, but her screech did not drown out the sound of a plane which was circling overhead.

I looked up, and hope leaped within me, for I recognized the machine, and as I rolled over again to avoid Eve's further attempts to grab me, Jake swooped down in a dive, and passed so low over us, that Eve and her brother instinctively ducked, and I took the opportunity to roll still further away from them.

For a second, they stood, wondering what to do, but when the plane banked and turned, and came down to within feet of the field, the man dropped Dirk on the ground and went racing across to the cliff path, while Eve dashed for her car.

TWENTY

The little plane came to a halt, and almost before the propeller blades had stopped turning, Jake was jumping to the ground, followed by Carlo. Before they could reach the spot where Dirk and I were lying, Eve, almost berserk with frustration, made one last attempt to get even with the man who had spurned her.

She started the car engine, sent the vehicle skidding in a tight circle, to come charging at full speed toward the spot where Dirk, who had recovered consciousness sprawled beside me.

Jake yelled a warning. Somehow Dirk struggled to his feet and dragged me away, only seconds before the car rocketed over the spot where we had been.

Eve braked, and again attempted to turn the car at speed, but this time she misjudged the maneouvre. The car skidded out of control, struck a rock, and somersaulted once, to land on its roof.

From the distance, as Carlo raced to free the trapped driver, we could hear the reassuring wail of police sirens. I knew, now, that the drama was coming to its end, and relief made me so weak that I could only lie helplessly on the ground, while Jake fumbled to undo the cords which bound me, muttering over and over again as he looked at my bruised face.

"Melissa, my darling! Are you all right? Are you all right?"

I could not restrain the tears which spilled from my eyes, any more than I could refrain from clinging to him, when the final bonds fell away, and he lifted me to my feet.

"Jake! Oh, Jake!" I buried my head against his shoulder. "How did you know where to come? Oh, Jake! You saved our lives!"

He did not reply, but only held me closer, as if afraid to let me go, and it was Carlo, who, after directing the police who had now arrived on the spot, to take care of Eve and her brother, answered for him.

"You told us where to come, Melissa!

"Yes," he went on. "It was you! When I found that the message I had received to go to the hospital was false, I broke all records to get back to the Villa Gelsomino. Then, when you didn't answer my ring, I broke down the door, and found, beside the telephone, your message, with all the doodles around it, doodles which told me where to make for, once I had gone next door in search of you and found the gate-keeper unconscious with the dogs lying poisoned at his side.

"You see, my dear," he explained, "scribbled around the message that you had gone next door, the word pink was repeated, and today's date, and coral, grotto, with question marks beside each word. Immediately I remembered how you had mentioned the Pink Grotto, wondering where you had heard about it, and things started to click into place.

"Jake arrived as I was taking off from the villa, having told the police where to make for, so we decided to come to your aid by air, for not only would it be quicker, but it would have the element of surprise."

"Carlo!" Jake interrupted firmly. "You can explain everything later. In the meantime, I am going to take Melissa to a doctor to have her cuts and bruises seen to," he touched my cheeks gently with his finger.

"She does look awful, doesn't she?" Dirk had recovered with surprising speed from the effects of the drug he had been given, and was standing beside us, not yet fully aware of all that had taken place, but full of excitement at the police activity, the hustle, the bustle, the attempts to pull Eve free, and even the sight of my battered self!

Jake looked down at my bruised and dirty cheeks, at my eyes sparkling with tears, at my tousled, grit filled hair.

"She looks beautiful!" he smiled at me with tenderness. "She always looks beautiful to me!"

Carlo laughed. "You see, Melissa!" he beamed. "I was right! But I wonder how much longer two pairs of eyes would have been blind to love, if this hadn't happened!" he shook his head.

I flushed, and moved away from Jake.

"Don't embarrass Jake, Carlo!" I pleaded.

"I am not embarrassed, my darling!" Jake continued to smile at me. "You know you have always been my favorite girl!"

"But what about Jane?" I asked. "She said—" I bit my lip and decided not to reveal what Jane had told me, but Jake was insistent.

"What did Jane say?" he asked.

"She said she was getting married when she re- turned home, to someone she was working with here—but it was a secret—and she wanted no one to know, especially Leo—and I thought," I looked at Jake despondently, "I was sure she meant you!"

Jake gaped. "Me?" he ejaculated in a startled tone.

Carlo flung his head back and laughed aloud, making the policemen who were standing nearby turn to look at us in puzzlement.

"Then, who?" I could not understand his denial.

"It is Max, you idiot!" Jake's smile re-appeared, and grew wider and wider. "Haven't you noticed how they are always together? And yet you thought," he went on, "that she meant me!"

"You darling little idiot!" he shook his head. "Is that why you have been behaving so oddly to- ward me, accepting flowers from strange men," he glanced at Carlo, remembering the moon dai- sies his friend had gathered for me, "keeping me at a distance? Melissa, Melissa," he sighed. "Don't you know you have always been my best girl, and that I was merely waiting for you to grow up, and spread your wings a little, before I asked you to marry me?"

He stood and looked at me, not touching me, not adding another word to what he had already said. I returned his gaze, gravely, unbelievingly at first. Then slowly, a smile of delight parted my lips, and we continued to stand for seconds longer, smiling at each other, unaware of the man and the boy standing looking at us with affectionate amusement, aware only of one another, and the wonder of the moment.

Jake was the first to move. He glanced around, and moved over to a small, flowering shrub, to snap from it a flowering twig. Laughingly he returned to me and tucked the blossom into the buttonhole of my crumpled shirt.

"Carlo gave you marguerites, moon daisies, for dreams, my darling, but I give you this," he touched the tiny, fragrant flowers. "This is the flower that every bride should carry on her wedding day; this is the flower you must have in your bouquet, my darling; myrtle, the flower of love; myrtle, more lasting than dream flowers," he took my hands and held them warmly in his, "Myrtle for my love!"